The Tarot Mysteries by Bevan Atkinson

The Emperor Card
The Empress Card
The High Priestess Card
The Magician Card
The Fool Card

THE FOOL CARD

THE FOOL.

A Tarot Mystery

by

Bevan Atkinson

Electra Enterprises of San Francisco

ISBN 978-0-9969425-0-8

Acknowledgements

Thanks first to my family, especially my mother Barbara, who dauntlessly supported every one of my creative endeavors, no matter how seemingly misguided or, more typically, expensive. Thanks to Lani Plonski for giving me my first tarot deck. Thanks also to early readers for their many helpful comments, particularly my true friend Barb Thompson. Thanks also to my sisters, cousins, and assorted family members (biological and in-law) who proofed, and to my novelist pal Duane Unkefer for information general and specific on how to write. When I asked him what the heck was the deal with all these voices clamoring in my head, he said, "Welcome to fiction, hon."

For Hubert Schwyzer

"...it is in pushing back against the world that a soul is defined."
Eliot Pattison, *Water Touching Stone*

≍׀≍

I lead a very quiet life, by intention. It is not yet a dotty old lady life, but I find eventfulness unpleasant.

A few months ago I was stretched out on the couch, with Katana curled up on the armrest behind my shoulders and Meeka purring next to my feet on the ottoman.

I was content. It was late at night, dark and foggy outside, and I had crushed lemon verbena and sage leaves into a salver. The fragrance was fresh but not distracting. I was rereading Nero Wolfe, enjoying Archie and the orchids and the shad roe dinners. Mr. Brubeck was playing soothing ballads.

The fog was in—it's pretty much always in on 48th Avenue—and the Monterey Cypresses in Sutro Park were looming shapes in the cold mist that flew past the big plate glass window. Waves boomed against Seal Rock.

Then came the thunk. It felt like a car had hit my house. Now, my house sits almost directly on the San Andreas Fault, so I am used to the occasional thunk that feels like a car has hit my house, followed by a few seconds of chink-chink-chink as the crockery rattles and the plant leaves quiver and the chandelier Fred Astaires elegantly back and forth, dancing on the ceiling.

This thunk was followed by the sound of a car door opening and footsteps scraping on the sidewalk. Damn. My house really *had* been hit by a car.

The cats, being cats, skittered for someplace low and dark. The two mongrels, Kinsey the small brown one and Hawk the large black one, stood up and trotted to the top of the stairs leading down to the front door. They looked attentively at me, Hamlet-like, for guidance. To bark or not to bark? The readiness is all.

Then the doorbell buzzed in an odd stutter and the dogs' question was no longer a question. They barreled downstairs, giving it the full Baskerville, and kept it up until I shouted "Quiet." They went quiet.

When I reached the ground floor landing, I peered out the window in the upper half of the door. Nobody there. I stood on tiptoe and could see a long leg extending down my two front steps into the circle of front door lamplight. There was a large buff suede work boot laced onto a big foot.

I deduced that someone, likely a male some-one, was sitting on my doorstep, leaning against the front door. It was either a one-legged some-one, or there was a second leg tucked up out of sight from my angle.

Beyond the leg was a black Porsche whose bumper had taken a chunk out of the stucco be-side my garage door. The house had taken a re-ciprocal chunk out of the Porsche.

"Who is it?" I spoke up, projecting my espe-cially no-nonsense tone of voice. Hawk huffed anxiously until I pointed at him. He stopped huff-ing.

"Please help me." I heard it, but only just. A deep hoarse voice.

"I asked who you are."

"Thorne Ardall."

"I'll call 911 and tell them to send an ambu-lance."

"*No!*" Now there was power in the voice.

"Mister, I don't know you, and I'm not open-ing the door. If you're hurt I'll call 911. That's it."

"Please. We have to hide the car. I'm not in any shape to protect you when he comes back."

"What do you mean, 'When he comes back'?"

"Because he will. Please. There's no time."

Well, there wasn't a reason in the world to trust him, and it was late at night and I live alone, so why in holy hell did I do what I did next? What I did was, I asked myself what to do and the answer was clear: "You can trust him, Child. Let him in and hide the car."

Here's the thing: I read tarot cards. I don't claim to be psychic or a witch or anything overly weird. I have just learned to trust the voice that calls me "Child." I leave you to draw the inevitable conclusion that I am another loony-tunes San Franciscan begging to be axe-murdered.

It's not much of a justification, but I count on the dogs to be protective, especially Hawk, and I have a history of taking in wounded-bird types and setting them back up on their pins. In the past they've been figuratively rather than literally wounded, but...

I pulled the door open and the big man nearly tipped over against my legs, then caught himself with his right hand and braced himself on the carpet. He held his left arm against his side.

The dogs rushed forward to sniff his face, which was higher than theirs even though he was sitting. They instantly backed off and snorted. Kinsey sneezed so hard her chin thwacked against the tile floor. I could smell blood as well as something off-putting; it was slightly chemical and made my nostrils want to shut.

I was gratified to find that my deduction about the other leg was correct. There it was, bent at the knee.

"Off," I said, and the dogs backed away and wagged their tails, stiff-legged and whining. Kinsey stretched her neck forward and sniffed the door, bloody where this guy who claimed to be the captain of the Kon-Tiki had leaned against it.

I looked down at a light yellow oxford-cloth shirt that was almost the same shade as his mop of hair. He neither looked up nor turned to look at me.

From the way he held himself, I deduced that twisting around was not something he wanted to do. So far I was doing some tippy-top deducing. And then I engaged in some more looniness—loony even by my standards, which we are already agreed are not standard at all.

"I'm going to let you in the garage," I said. "There's a room in the back we can use to check out how badly you're hurt. I can't guarantee I won't call an ambulance." I pressed the garage door button and the door began to rise.

"Thank you." As he said this he seemed to relax. Or maybe he was collapsing.

"Where are your car keys?" I put out my hand.

"The ignition." He pulled himself to his feet, groaning as he unbent and struggled for balance. Finally he turned to look in my direction, his face shadowed as he bent forward, not making eye contact. He braced his right arm against the door frame.

"Are you going to make it without help? I'll need a derrick if you can't keep yourself upright." Now that he was standing I could see he was more than big; he was middle linebacker size, six-foot-six or -eight, and not frail.

I'm not frail either, but I top out at five-nine and less than half this guy's weight. I'm blonde too, but I pay Mr. Trevor major bucks every month and sit for hours looking like a microwave tower in order to achieve a color this man had factory-installed.

I squelched my hair-color envy when I saw there was a bloodstain glistening across his shirt, broadest where his arm was pressed against his left side. He turned and stepped slowly into the garage, dragging his feet a little as he passed my lovely blue Chrysler 300C and headed toward the door leading from the garage to the downstairs guest room.

"There's a bathroom. Use the towels and I'll be there as soon as I pull your car in," I called to him.

"Stay," I told the dogs as I curled myself into the Porsche. It had stalled in second gear. I slid the seat forward three or four feet, stepped on the clutch, started the car, pressed the gearshift down into reverse and gave it a little gas.

The tires chirped as I rocketed directly toward Eileen and Henry Chung's new silver Lexus SUV across the street. Slamming my feet on the brake and the clutch, I shifted into first gear and tried giving the Porsche a little less gas. I remembered my Dad saying "when you're on the freeway you don't drive; you aim," so I aimed at the garage, knowing that in this car I could reach freeway speed in first gear. Houses in San Francisco sit on long, narrow lots, and if you have two cars you park them in tandem. The demon car chirped to a halt three inches from the Chrysler's rear bumper.

Modestly triumphant, I climbed out and went to get the dogs and shut the front door. They skittered past me as I picked up the chunk of stucco and set it down on the concrete floor of the garage. I pushed the Genie button to slide the door down behind me.

Now to see if my unexpected guest had bled to death in my brand-new guest bath. This was an event, no doubt about it, and I found it curious that it didn't feel unpleasant.

Not at all. No indeed.

≈2≈

He was sitting on the edge of the deep tub with his shirt off. I could see clumps of muscles all over his upper body. I might have found this appealing if I hadn't been appalled by the gruesome shirt he had pressed up against his side, and the brown-red patches of dried blood on his skin. He had rolled his shirt up and was pressing it against both his back and a spot on his abdomen below his ribs. The dogs went up to him and sniffed.

"Out," I told the dogs, and they stepped away from the shoji screens that divide the bathroom from the bedroom. "Sit." They planted their rear ends on the tatami matting. I knew this situation was getting to them, because they were doing exactly what I told them to do, the first time I told them to do it.

I turned to my guest. "Let me see," I said. He lifted the shirt and I saw two holes in his skin.

"Jesus. I thought you were hurt in the accident. Have you been shot?"

"Yes. The bleeding is slowing down. I passed out. That's why I ran into your house." He was looking down at his side.

"Okay, this is way more than I can handle. You need a doctor right now."

"No doctor," he said, keeping his eyes down.

"Please listen to me. What I know how to do is smear a little goop on a cut and cover it with a Band-Aid. What if something vital is bleeding internally? What if there's infection or the bullet is still in there? I'd like to help you, but this is nuts."

I was wondering why he wouldn't make eye contact. Con men generally make eye contact a part of their pitch. This man was not pleading; he was simply stating facts.

"The bullet went through. Just muscle."

"Why no doctor? You're very badly hurt. I can't begin to do the right thing with this kind of wound."

He looked up at me. Dark green, flecked with brown and yellow, his eyes were startling, with dark brown eyelashes and eyebrows. "There would be police. No police." Now that he had finally looked at me, he didn't look away.

"Why not?" I asked. "What kind of trouble are you in?"

He didn't answer me. We stared at each other for a few seconds. I realized three things: one, he had a decision-making process I was not invited to participate in; two, I didn't believe he was a dangerous criminal; three, the back of my slacks and sweater where they had touched the Porsche's driver's seat must be as bloody as his shirt. I sighed.

"Here's the deal, thunder god. Tell me what's going on or I'm out. Trust me entirely or not at all."

His eyes looked down, and he was quiet, thinking. He looked up at me. He had decided.

"It's Thorne, not Thor. I don't exist," he said. Shot and bloody, he was quick enough to get my dumb Nordic god joke.

"Keep going. What do you mean by 'you don't exist'?"

"I'm off the grid. Try to find me and you will strike out."

"Why?"

He sighed, as if the answer was obvious and I was testing his patience. "To have an identity is to be tracked and monitored and marketed to and taxed and junk-mailed, jury-dutied, spammed. I don't want that. I'm not a criminal in the sense most people mean. But I don't pay taxes. I don't vote. I don't have a driver's license or a social security number or a 401(k). I haven't seen or spoken with my parents in fifteen years. I don't have an address or a listed phone number."

"How do you live? How do you drive a car like that?"

"People pay me cash. I buy things with cash.

The car belongs to Victor Avery. I was his body-guard. I lived where he lived."

"If you're not working for him anymore, why do you still have the car?"

"He died tonight." He paused and corrected himself. "He was killed tonight. I was following the killer. In the Presidio I pulled up alongside the other car, a silver Jaguar, and the driver shot me."

He smiled slightly and shook his head, looking up at me again. "I made it this far, but I passed out for a second."

"And ran into my house," I said. He nodded.

"Who was driving the Jag?" I asked.

He shook his head no. Oh swell. An unknown armed assailant is now in my future. I don't need my cards to tell me that. I wish cards could give me five quick tips on fending off flying bullets.

I found myself in a strange state of mind, not really thinking or reacting; I had passed the threshold of astonishment and logical thought processes had ceased.

So I changed the subject. "How are you doing? Do you feel like you're going to pass out again?"

"No."

"All right. I'm going to call my friend Patrick and ask him what to do."

Thorne raised his eyebrows.

"No, he won't blab. He's going to tell me how to treat the wound. And I'm going to bring you some tea."

"Tea?"

"Yes, tea. I don't know jack about gunshot wounds, but I'm utterly competent with tea. Are you going to be all right for a few minutes?"

"Yes." More steady eye contact. "What is your name?"

"Rosalind Alexandra Bard, but I go by Xana. *Enchantée.*"

He held out a big hand and mine disappeared inside it. His skin was papery but not rough, and his grasp was steady and purposeful. He didn't use the garbage-compactor grip some men think is manly, but there was no question that this was a man shaking my hand. A short jittery laugh escaped me as we observed this little ritual. I don't think I was in complete control of my behavior. I don't imagine anyone would disagree with me on that.

"Listen. The dogs are harmless unless I sic them on something, and then they're trouble. Stay here if you would, please."

He nodded. I went and sat down on the low platform bed and called Patrick Dennehy. He's married to one of my many long-distance friends, in this case my first roommate when I moved to San Francisco. Kauai Kalitzky met Patrick, who was a Major in the Army Nurse Corps stationed at Pearl Harbor, when she went to Hawaii on vacation.

Patrick works nights in an emergency room outside Montpelier, Vermont, where he moved after being busted for marijuana possession eighteen months before he was eligible to retire from the Army.

He had explained that staying loaded every non-working hour was the only way he could see his way clear to completing the twenty years necessary to retire.

"Isn't irony a bitch?" he said when he was forced to resign his commission. "That irony shit will straighten a soldier right the fuck out."

It was after midnight back east. I hoped Patrick would be working and available, and he was.

"Ex-anna-fanna-fo-fanna! How are you, babycakes! To what do I owe this pleasure?"

Patrick, being at work, was not loaded, but for him the Sixties never die. Patrick's conversational style runs the gamut from doo-wop to army slang to Irish blarney to unintelligible stoner munchy snarfles.

"Hello, my dear. I have a serious medical question and I know you will not give me any crap about being unable to give medical advice over the phone, and I know that you will tell me if you're busy and can't do this now, and I also know that you will not give me a ration of attitude about what I'm going to ask, and that you will keep your mouth shut about this with everybody but the lovely Miz KayKay."

"What have you gone and gotten yourself into this time, you little minx?"

"Okay or not okay, sweetie? You know I

wouldn't call at this hour with all these require-
ments if it weren't a big deal."

He snapped into true-blue friend mode.
"Okay, okay, sure thing. Go."

"How do I treat a through-and-through gunshot wound that has almost stopped bleeding.
The bullet entered…"

"*Whoa whoa whoa!*"

"…the front left torso about two inches above
the waist and about three-fourths of the way between his middle and his side, and exited out the
back about an inch from his side. The space between the two holes is about four inches and it's
below his ribs. I'm sorry I don't know all the ante-
rior and dorsal and epidermis words."

"Xana, I'm not kidding, this is not funny. He
has to go to the hospital right now. It's likely the
bullet hit the intestine or the liver, depending on
which side."

"He won't go, Patrick, or I would already
have taken him. And it's his left side, so I don't
think it's his liver."

"What kind of a wacko is this guy? It's a gunshot wound. You will land in a colossal world of
shit if you are caught not reporting this, not to
mention the minor consideration that he could die
if he doesn't get medical treatment from somebody who knows exactly what to do."

"Patrick, help me or don't, okay sweetie? I
love you and I get it that you are trying to keep
me safe from badness, but tell me how to treat the

wound or I'm going to hang up and clean it with some spit on a Kleenex."

"Christ on a cracker with cream cheese," he moaned. "All right, I'll tell you what to do and then I'll say a prayer for you both because you're going to need all the prayers you can get. But first, is the bullet still in him? If it is, there's nothing for it but to get him to a doctor. If he won't go willingly, I recommend you employ the Louisville Slugger anesthetic."

"He says no, it went clean through and it's probably in his car."

"All right then, let's of course believe the man. My God, I thought you swore off guys like this." He heard me sigh. "I'm sorry, that wasn't nice. Forgive me. Okay, here we go. Are you ready? Are you going to freak out cleaning up the wound and the blood?"

I reminded him that it's been my experience that more boys than girls are freaked out about blood, and he began to explain purposefully about sterile gauze and erythromycin and sutures and hemostats and pressure bandages, and when I told him how very humorous he was, he shifted to Plan B.

I put the phone on speaker and Thorne and I worked with cotton make-up remover pads and rubbing alcohol and paper towels and Polysporin and that strappy white mailing tape you have to cut with a blowtorch.

He grabbed the edge of the sink the first time I

touched the wound with alcohol, but he stayed conscious and followed the instructions as Patrick gave them. Almost immediately the mystery man and I were working smoothly in concert, no talking required. We both knew it, and we both said nothing about it. We managed to mop all the blood off and bandage him up rather neatly, all things considered.

The dogs were fascinated and a constant source of moral support, leaning forward every so often and sniffing up bad germs.

"Is there any more bleeding visible on the paper towels?" Patrick asked. We had used folded paper towels and the mailing tape in lieu of gauze and pressure bandages.

"No."

"Then the bullet must have missed the big arteries and veins. Let's hope it missed the big nerves as well. Give him fluids and iron tablets and eight hundred milligrams of ibuprofen every six hours, not that it will make much difference. He's going to hurt in ways he won't have words to describe. He should have antibiotics but you aren't getting those without a doctor."

He nattered on some more about painful scarring and changing bandages and making the patient rest and the risk of reopening the wound, and we were done.

"You're a god, Patrick. Bless you."

"A flawed, mortal deity to be doing such a misguided thing as this, minx-girl. I might have to call tomorrow and check up on you, you know."

"That would be nice. I love our chats, even when they don't involve bullets. Bye, sweetie. Give my love to KayKay."

I helped the big man get to his feet and to the bed. My help consisted of watching carefully as he braced his right arm on the edge of the tub and hoisted himself up, and then following behind him, dwarfed by his shadow as he walked. He was alert, but I felt like he was only just hanging on.

I pulled down the duvet and he sat so I could kneel down and unlace his boots and pull them off.

"That's it for the disrobing assistance," I said.

His mouth curved up into a little smile and he swung his legs into the bed, leaning against the pillows and headboard. I covered his legs with the duvet.

"I like this room," he said, looking around. "It's beautiful."

I think the room is beautiful too. I took a lot of care to make it calm and serene, with lots of white and taupe and pale wood and celadon-colored porcelain containers full of blooming orchids that I foofed with misted water every morning.

On a table under the window that looked out on the carefully lit Japanese garden was a massive white Phalaenopsis orchid with fourteen butter-plate-sized blossoms weighing down its curving stem. The air smelled of the cinnamon sticks and cloves I'd put in a little cloisonné dish by the bed.

"Thank you," he said, looking down at his hands. There were dark lines of dried blood crusted under the fingernails of the left one.

"You're welcome," I replied, ever the well brought up daughter of Louisa Duncan Livingston Monaghan Bard of Darien, Connecticut. "I'm going to make the tea now."

The dogs followed me upstairs while I brewed fresh chamomile and mint tea using the herbs I grow in tubs on my deck, and they followed me downstairs as I carried the tray with the teapot and strainer and mug and painkillers and bowlful of iron-enriched cereal and milk and a big spoon and a tea towel for a napkin.

Seven years after my last romantic exploit, seven years after swearing off ever again rescuing some poor unemployed but smart, funny, literate, sexy basket case only to put him successfully up on his feet so he could walk out on me, I had throttled up at warp speed into full wounded-bird repair mode.

The inner me was blissful. My therapist was going to have a cow. All my friends were going to have cows. My mother was definitely going to have a cow. They could start a goddamn dairy farm for all I cared.

א א א

It was after midnight by the time I went down to

the guest room with the cereal and the tea. Thorne had fallen asleep. No snoring or tooth-gnashing or muttering; only stillness and slow, steady breathing. The two black cats were curled up into each other on one side of his long legs. I don't let pets on my bed and they don't sleep in my bedroom with me. Thunder god apparently had no such scruples, or maybe he was out cold at the time of the cat incursion.

I left the tea and the cereal on the nightstand and headed up to my bedroom. I could hear the dogs jumping up on the duvet as I went up the stairs.

This man was the size of a diesel locomotive, so even though it would form no real deterrent, I locked my bedroom door. He was asleep and had lost half his blood and was probably too weak to climb two flights of stairs to get to me, but still I locked the door. I had let him in my house willingly even though I live alone and it was late at night, but I locked the door.

Loony tunes.

I unlocked the door.

I stood and stared sightlessly at my room for a moment. Then I walked over to the inlaid rosewood box and took out my tarot cards.

I don't read cards for a living or anything, but I've studied them for many years, and when they're not available I've relied on the intuition that the cards have trained in me. In this way I get access to information many people ignore.

I can tell whether or not a bus is going to get to my stop within the next five minutes. If I'm driving, I can usually find my way without a GPS system telling me the right turn is approaching in one hundred yards.

I can tell a lot about someone or something by asking myself an internal question and waiting for the answer. Sometimes I get one and proceed accordingly; sometimes I don't and I use my judgment, for good or ill. But when I've ignored the answers (and occasional unsolicited promptings) from the voice that calls me "Child," it's invariably proved regrettable.

You can think of it as answered prayers, if it makes you more comfortable with the quote occult unquote. I don't really care whether you're comfortable with it or not. Tonight I had asked what I should do about the wounded man on my doorstep, and the voice had called me "Child" and told me to trust the guy.

So I did. There you go.

≈3≈

Down in the guest room I moved orchids off a teak table and pulled the table over to the bed-side. My guest was still lights-out and the paper towel bandages continued to hold the fort.

Meeka and Katana were purring in their sleep, Kinsey was flicking her paws in a dream, and Hawk lay watching me with his chin resting on Thorne's knee.

The lamp on the nightstand cast a muted glow across the bed. I unwrapped the silk scarves that protect my cards. The scarves smell of the san-dalwood that lines the rosewood box they live in. Unwrapping the cards, placing the scarves on a table and inhaling the sandalwood scent are steps I take each time to silence my conscious thoughts and prepare to listen to my intuition. The cards, when I first unwrap them, are always cool to the touch.

I brought over a chair, sat down, and worked with the deck for a while, shuffling and pressing it into the palms of my hands, warming the chilly cards up and clearing my mind.

When the deck felt ready, I cut it three times and sat waiting until I had the urge to use the pile on the right. I recombined the cards, putting the right-hand pile on top, and laid out a left-to-right sequence of five cards.

Left-most was the King of Pentacles reversed. In tarot-speak, "reversed" means upside down. To the King's right was the Ten of Swords. In the center was the Fool Card, his number a Zero. Next was the Queen of Cups reversed, followed by the Princess of Wands reversed.

One thing: the cards are pieces of cardboard with pictures on them, okay? They're not magical or eerie or wicked. They can't foretell the future and they aren't meant to be used to scare your college friends at keggers. Learning to read them is a little like learning to interpret dreams. To study tarot is to study all the metaphysical "sciences" it integrates: astrology, numerology, kabbalah, color symbology, and many others. One story is that Carl Jung based his theory of archetypes on the tarot deck's imagery.

The tarot deck is a tool, a window, an invitation into the place where lives the connection we all have to wisdom and truth, or the universal unconscious, or whatever you decide to call it. However you arrive at the conviction that there's more to all this than you thought, it's the same experience for all of us once we get there.

A tarot deck is divided into the Major and Minor Arcana; some people think the Fool Card is a third group all to itself. The Major Arcana consist of twenty-two cards; the Minor Arcana of fifty-six cards in four suits that each run from Ace through King and are the precursors to the playing cards we use today. The only card from the Major Arcana to remain in the modern deck is the Fool, or, as he's now called, the Joker.

Having the Fool appear at the center of the layout was a surprise. He doesn't show up often, and when he does it's usually a warning to strap yourself in for a thrill ride. Something new and different and potentially very risky is in the offing.

Brief images flashed across my mind's eye: a blonde, well-kept but no longer fresh-faced, and a tall dark-haired man with dark eyes who struck me as full of dignity and power. There was another man as well, but I couldn't get a clear image of him. I sensed tension, stress, disharmony. The words "lord of ether" came to me; it's one of the Fool Card's sobriquets.

As I looked at the Princess of Wands card I saw a dark-haired younger woman. In her hands were smoke and silvery metal or foil, and I felt an oppressive but muted anger.

I'm a night owl. I had no worries about watching over Thorne until morning, but suddenly I wanted to know what news, if any, had reached the media about the death he claimed had occurred.

I pulled the edges of the scarves up over the cards and crossed the room to the cabinet where a little flat-screen television lived. I turned it on and muted it, surfing through the channels until I found one with a local news update. I moved closer and raised the volume until I could barely hear it.

"*...was apparently killed earlier tonight in an explosion at his Presidio Terrace home. Neighbors heard the explosion and called firefighters, who controlled the resulting blaze just before midnight. Mr. Avery's wife and daughter were not at home at the time of the explosion, the cause of which is unknown. Full details on our morning edition at six.*"

I switched off the TV and turned to my guest, who stared sadly at the blank screen and then looked at me.

"I'm sorry I woke you," I whispered. "You should sleep some more. I'll pour you some tea. It will help you sleep."

"I need to find Victor's killer."

I considered the straightforward, unequivocal way he'd said that, walked around the bed, poured him some tea and handed it to him, and asked "Who are the stressed-out people? The tall dark, dignified man and the blonde thirty-something woman who wears bright colors?"

"Victor and Sally."

"Drink some tea." He sipped. I needed more information.

"Do you ever speak in compound sentences?" I asked.

He looked at me. "Sometimes I do and sometimes I don't," he said.

I admit I laughed. Grammar jokes are my Achilles heel. I hoped he would open up once I started asking specific questions.

"The news mentioned a daughter. Is she reckless perhaps? A little out of control? Or maybe insensitive in some way? No, it's more than that. Does she use drugs?"

"Natalie. Victor's daughter. Victor caught her freebasing last month. She ran away from home last year. Victor brought her home from New Orleans. How can you know about her?" Thorne was frowning.

"This may sound stupid, but does the word 'ether' mean anything in association with this family?"

"Victor runs Avery Chemical. They produce ether."

"For what? I thought nobody used ether nowadays, not since they came up with better anesthetics."

"Solvents. Illegal drugs."

"One more question. What new enterprise or major change was Victor embarked on? Maybe something involving his wife or some other family member? Maybe a man? Or someone jealous?"

"Victor's brother Ellis. How the hell do you know all this?"

"I said it wasn't easy to explain. I was using my intuition."

I sat down beside the bed and he saw the scarves on the table. The edge of one card was visible. He reached for it.

"Don't touch them, please," I said, and he heard my tone and dropped his hand to the duvet, where it landed on Meeka. She jolted awake. He scratched her ears gently and she pushed her head against his fingers and purred so loudly she buzzed like an electric pencil sharpener. He sipped some tea. He looked at the rest of the animals and then at me.

"Fishies? Parakeets? Boa constrictors?" he said. "A tame tarantula?"

"I know, I know." I held my hand up to forestall any further comments about the menagerie.

"Tell me," he said, pointing at the scarves.

"I use tarot cards to figure things out when I need more insight than I can manage unassisted. Sometimes I see images when I read them. I saw images of the people I was asking about."

"Ah." He nodded as if that was all he needed to know. I was surprised. Most people don't stop with "Ah" and a nod.

"If it makes you uncomfortable I'll put them away."

"No, no. Tap into all worlds corporeal and incorporeal." There was the flicker of a smile again.

"Tell me what happened tonight?"

"Victor was killed."

"Why do you think so? Besides the fact that someone shot you, of course."

"Someone was in the house tonight."

"You were at the house?"

"I was always where Victor was."

"Wait a minute. That chemical smell on your clothes. Was that ether?"

"Yes. I was in my room at the house. The explosion knocked me over. I ran to the library but there was no way in through the flames. I could see that Victor was..." He stopped. For a moment I wasn't in my guest room anymore; I was standing looking at a jumble of shelves and flames and books and leather furniture, and a man's horribly mangled body.

"He was dead." Thorne went on, and I was in the blood-spattered room with him. "I could smell ether. I heard Sally's Jaguar and I ran to the garage. But Sally wasn't home so I don't know who was driving it."

I changed the subject. "Why did Victor hire you?"

He thought about that for a few seconds. "I take care of people," he said, setting his mug down on the tray. This man's movements struck me as thoughtful, necessary, precise.

"Meaning?"

"Construe that as you will." He aimed his level gaze at me. It took no time at all to think of a way to construe it that led me to wonder again what I was doing hosting this fellow in my guest room. I looked over at Hawk, who now seemed to be wearing an "I-told-you-so" expression on his lean, intelligent face.

"How did Mr. Avery come to need such a special caretaker?" I asked, steering clear of any explicit construing for now.

"I've known Victor since prep school."

"That doesn't answer my question. Why did he need you?"

He sighed. Grief dragged down his face.

"He needed someone better than me," he said quietly, pulling his hand away from the cat, crossing his arms on his chest and closing his eyes. Meeka lifted her head and looked up at him, her purring interrupted. It was so quiet I could hear the air in my ears. I waited and watched as Thorne pretended to sleep, and then did sleep.

I uncovered and looked at the cards again. I was sure the first two, the King of Pentacles and the frightening Ten of Swords, dealt with tonight's death. The Queen of Cups and Princess of Wands seemed to be about Mrs. Avery and her daughter Natalie.

But face cards can also refer to events, not just people. These could be interpreted to mean lost wealth, misguided efforts, emotional manipulation, or a sequence of miserable, numbing personal woes. Thorne's comments made me wonder how ambiguous the cards were being. The Reader and the Querent, or requestor, have to work as a team to interpret them.

The Fool card is always a conundrum. The zero attributed to him is all and nothing at all. The Fool implies opposites: the cycle of all experience and the great unknowable; knowledge and tomfoolery; the beginning of a bountiful and fulfilling enterprise or an embarkation on a futile and ill-advised misadventure.

In most readings the Querent feels the information is specifically for him or her. But I know from experience that for me as well there's something to learn in every layout of the cards.

I asked myself why was the Fool sitting there, the fulcrum in the middle of the layout? What were the Averys and Thorne embarking on? What was I embarking on? I thought it had to do with my hard-earned aversion to eventfulness.

Not long before this I had let the responsible parties on high know that, in spite of my aversion, I was prepared for the next major event in my life, whatever it might be. And then I prayed they wouldn't take me up on it.

But *voilà*, here I was looking at the Fool Card after a major event crashed into my house. Not a subtle clue from the guys upstairs, but, as was once said of the Titanic, I have a lot of power and not a lot of rudder. Something was steering me toward this experience.

Okay then, first things first. I was going to get this man well enough to venture out into the world and see what we could learn about Victor Avery's murder. Thorne's situation was mine to mess around with for now and I was anxious to get started, safely in my power position, fixing somebody else's problems rather than my own.

With luck, maybe I'd fix one or two problems of mine along the way, but that was merely a nice-to-have.

Barefoot, I padded upstairs in the dark to make more tea, this time for myself. I left the lights off, because I like to pad around my house in the dark and because the streetlight from the corner shines straight into my kitchen. Even on foggy nights I can see the electric teakettle and faucet just fine.

As I waited for the water to boil I gazed out at the silent, fog-shrouded street. I heard a car engine, then saw mist-blurred headlights creeping slowly along Anza Street toward my corner. A silver Jaguar XJS convertible, top up, stopped under the light at the corner. I could read the car's license plate: AVERY4, but the fog obscured whoever was behind the wheel.

The car, pointed at the front of my house, turned on its high beams and the hair on my forearms prickled. Could I be seen? I stood frozen, afraid any movement would be visible. Had I remembered to lock the front door? It would lock automatically after I shut it, but I hadn't thrown the deadbolt.

Why would the killer wait so long to retrace

his route? I was ready to jump to the phone and call 911 if anyone climbed out of the car.

But no one did. The Jaguar turned onto 48th Avenue and slid elegantly past my house, the tail-lights fading as it drove away.

I had been going to make Darjeeling tea, thinking that for the coming all-nighter caffeine would be a good idea. I replaced the loose black tea leaves in their container and pulled out the chamomile and mint. I had come upstairs thinking I would need help staying awake all night. Now I needed help stifling the adrenaline that had my hands shaking as I poured boiling water into a clean teapot.

≍4≍

Birds were tweeting when Thorne awoke. I had finished with Archie and Saul and Fritz and Theodore during the night and was reading Kate Ross's *The Devil in Music*. My tarot cards were folded into their scarves and tucked into their rose- and sandalwood box upstairs.

"How are you feeling?" I asked him.

"Like I've been shot," he said. He lifted his long arms over his head to stretch and his breath blew out of him in a surprised gasp. He dropped his arms down and managed a yawn without hurting himself any more.

"There's cereal if you're hungry. Or I could cook something, please say not to bother."

I said that because I don't cook. Or rather, I do cook when cooking is unavoidably obligatory, but I don't much care for the activity.

"Please don't bother."

"Everything's there on the tray. Help yourself. I don't know why people can't send out for breakfast like they can for lunch and dinner."

He poured cereal in the bowl, added milk, and started eating.

"I brought down a toothbrush and all that and put it in the bathroom for you, but I don't think you should be on your feet very much until you've healed a little."

"I'll be fifteen minutes," he said in that snarfy way you do when, no matter how genteelly you try to eat it, your lower jaw is jutting forward trying to keep the milk and cereal in your mouth.

"Please don't go. I have this idea. I'd like to know what you plan to do about Mr. Avery's murder, and be part of the plan. Please. I know it's none of my business, but I feel like it is a little bit because the silver Jaguar came back and stopped in front of the house…"

"When? Did you see the driver?" He was focused on me like I was some sort of prey.

"Around one-thirty, and no, I didn't see who it was." I told him about the license plate. "If anyone had climbed out of the car I'd have called the police. But the car stayed there for a few seconds and then drove up Forty-Eighth Avenue toward Geary."

"Again with the cops?" he said.

"But I didn't call them. Listen, I've been thinking about this all night." He looked at my index finger holding the page open half-way through my book. "Most of the night. Please let me help you? Let me investigate and be ambulatory while you're on the mend? Please? I can't explain why this is so important to me, but it is. And you've seen already that I can be very—call it 'insightful' about things."

"That was uncanny." He lifted the bowl and looked down at his bandage. He rested his big hand on it and then began spooning cereal into his mouth again.

"Is that a yes? Am I in?" I asked.

"Why? Most people would run from this."

"It's hard to explain. I just know I'm supposed to be part of finding out what happened."

"Weird."

"I suppose one might think so, if one were not me. I think I'm perfectly normal."

"Why would anyone involved tell you anything?"

"I'm guessing you're the one they won't be willing to talk to. I get the feeling you don't let people get very close. I don't think most folks would talk freely to someone as scary as you. With me it's the opposite. They blab everything. I sit quietly and nod my head and say 'oh my,' and I ask questions and they uncork. If I weren't bristling with so much integrity I could make a sumptuous living as a blackmailer."

"You're leaving something out."

I couldn't hold his stare. "It's a long story," I

said, praying he had a short attention span.

"Once upon a time," he prompted.

So I told him.

Eighteen months ago I had been fired, and being fired had not happened to me before. I had been director of a key department in a high-tech start-up company, and my charge was to do the impossible by two days ago. So I did it.

I had a team of ten marvelously creative and good-humored people working for me, and we were the subject of glowing business magazine articles. But once we'd launched our product and it was a massive success, the venture capitalists threw a vitriolic cost-cutting Chief Operating Officer into the mix, "to focus on maximum return on investment," they said.

My budget offended her, so she started in on me. Her abuse was administered brutally and in public. I assume she hoped I would buckle and walk away quietly and cheaply. Somewhat to my surprise, I discovered I am not a buckle-and-walk-away-quietly person. I told her to stop, documented everything she did, and sent the documentation to my own managers as well as to the folks in HR and Legal. I knew nobody would stand up and help me; they were more scared of her than I was.

When she told me I was "laid off" after eight excruciating months, I toted all the print-outs to a labor lawyer and six months later I was handed an enormous check. Yippee skippy, right? Oh, I wish. It shook me up hard and set me down rattled.

I know: waa-waa, take the money and stop whining. I'm not sorry it happened. This was my personal employment hell; everybody's gone through one, and I'm describing, not regretting it.

When the parts reassembled themselves I was a different person. I can no longer be what I do for a living. I have to be who I am and let that be enough. We all have to learn this lesson at some point, and I'm a little late to the party, I admit. I'm adjusting. I'm not sure I'll ever learn how to be proud of myself without endorsers.

I told Thorne that after the tears dried and I had read three hundred books in a year, redecorated my house and garden from top to bottom, spent hours and hours in therapy, and lost thirty pounds, I had notified the powers that be about my readiness for whatever was next in store for me. The readiness is all.

"And here you are," I finished, "and I believe you and the Averys are what's next in store. Plus the dogs and the cats like you. I'm taking that as a sign that you're a nice person, rather than a sucker who'll let them get up on the bed with you because you don't have the fortitude to say no and mean it in the face of their manipulative, pleading stares."

He didn't say anything. I didn't say anything. He reached for the sleeping Meeka and stroked her side. She jolted up mewing, licked his hand, purred, and put her head down.

"You do nothing without checking with me first," he said. "It's all trust all the time or, as you so succinctly put it, I'm out."

I smiled. It was a big smile, too. I was glad my parents had sprung for orthodontia and then made me wear my retainer. As I showed off my expensive teeth I think my face might have turned pink.

≂**5**≂

"Tell me more about the Averys," I said, after Thorne had brushed his teeth and sponged himself clean and changed the bandages. Patrick had forbidden a shower. Thorne's chin and neck were covered with dark stubble; apparently my pink cushiony razor was unappealing. He was stretching out the size 2X T-shirt I wear when I take long walks with the dogs.

We were sitting upstairs in the kitchen and I had more tea. Thorne had coffee. The dogs had kibble. The cats were up on the refrigerator eating kitty crunchies.

"I've known Victor since we were at Choate and then Princeton. He went to work for his dad. I disappeared."

"Why disappear after Princeton? Most people don't go to Princeton to become invisible afterward."

"My parents wanted Wall Street for me. I was at Harvard, getting an MBA. My uncle and I were close, and when he died he left me everything he had, which was a lot. Suddenly I could do whatever I wanted. I decided to walk away. My parents were furious."

"Are your parents still alive?"

"I haven't heard otherwise."

"You have no contact at all?"

"Not for many years."

"They must be worried about you."

"Not about me. About being an esteemed, old-money family, yes." There wasn't any bitterness in his tone, only a matter-of-fact assessment of how he saw things. "The best house, the best car, the best suburb and school and company. The best charity, for Christ's sake," he laughed. "Everything but what I wanted for me."

"They haven't tried to contact you?"

"How could they?" he said.

"Okay," I said. "But if you liquidated the estate there must have been some residue. What happened to that?"

"I keep a safe in a storage unit."

"But if you're storing cash in it rather than investing you're losing money every day."

"Ah, the little capitalist?" he snorted. "Who said I was storing cash?"

"Then what?"

"Gold."

"*What*!? You have a safe full of *gold*?"

"Semi-full."

"But why?"

"Because gold prices increase in line with inflation. Because gold is easy to buy and sell, takes less space than currency, and doesn't suffer from crazy economic policies."

"It sounds awfully complicated."

"It's simpler than you think. Go on-line and take a look. It's easy to trade precious metal. The basic process is the same as buying a pair of socks."

"Criminy." It was hard to fathom; I was dealing with a Scrooge McDuck, who stored his wealth in a money bin instead of in some financial institution's mainframe computer.

I took a different tack. "When did you start working for Victor?"

"Two months ago."

"How did that come about?"

"My previous client retired. When a job ends I make phone calls. I called Victor to say hello and he hired me."

"Why?"

"He said the long-lost Ellis had shown up. Victor said Ellis was a threat."

"Where had Ellis been? You say Ellis was long-lost. Why was it a threat when he showed up?"

"Nobody had heard from him for years. He wasn't a very good guy."

"How was he not a good guy?"

"Disowned. Victor called him a lost cause."

"Why would Victor need you when Ellis re-appeared?"

"Ellis was cleaned up and looked prosperous. He said he wanted to re-establish the connection. Victor said he didn't trust Ellis. There was bad blood."

"Bad blood how?"

"Because Victor got Avery Chemical and Ellis got the boot. He got in trouble and disappeared. While Ellis was nowhere to be found, the parents were killed in a car wreck. Victor had been working in the business for ten years by then and he assumed his father's job. Victor controls fifty-one percent of the stock, but somehow Ellis has acquired a lot of stock. He may be able to force Victor to give him a seat on the Board."

"How long ago did Ellis show up?"

"Right before I called Victor."

"What does Ellis do for a living?"

"He says seafood manufacturing. My guess is he likes to go fishing."

"How is Ellis acquiring shares?"

"I don't know. I've heard that he's offering the other board members inflated prices for their shares."

"Wouldn't they risk being liable in some way if they sold? Insider trading or something?"

"Probably not. They could argue that it was a fiduciary responsibility to the shareholders to boost the stock price."

"Where do you fit into all this?"

"Victor said Ellis had threatened him."

"Physically?"

"Yes."

"How? By beating him up, shooting him, what?"

"Nothing specific—a 'you'll be sorry' kind of thing. But Victor thought Ellis might try something. My job was to prevent it."

"How?"

"Weapons, hand-to-hand, martial arts, surveillance, security equipment, monitoring, evasive driving. Personal security in its many guises." He thought about what he'd said for a moment before going on. "Last night has me baffled. Victor wasn't supposed to permit anyone around him without my knowing about it. But someone was there with him. I need to look at the security video."

"There's video?"

"There's video."

"Tell me about the rest of the family," I said.

"Sally is younger than Victor. Not a lot."

"How did they meet?"

"Why?"

"I have no idea. I'm just asking about everything because I don't know what matters and what doesn't."

"At some business event. She had a young daughter, Natalie. They married pretty quickly."

"What's Sally like?"

Thorne thought about that. "Tough. Organized. Difficult to read sometimes. Beautiful. A hard worker. Disciplined. She doesn't flirt."

"Why do you mention flirting?"

He stared at me, the "duh" stare.

"Oh, I see. What about the daughter?"

"A problem. Acts out. Drugs. She does flirt, and not in a good way."

"She's seventeen, you said. Where is she in school?"

"Sacred Heart. She's cutting classes."

Convent of the Sacred Heart on upper Broadway is where rich Catholic families send their destined-to-be-rich Catholic daughters.

In a city that's essentially one hundred fifty-some years old, that started out jammed full of Spanish and Irish and Italian immigrants, Sacred Heart and Saint Ignatius and the University of San Francisco are where you send your children if you want them to become the local aristocracy when they grow up. Almost every mayor in the city's history has gone to those schools.

"What have Victor and Sally done about Natalie so far?"

"Worry. Since she came home they thought they had her back on the straight and narrow. Last month Victor caught her doing coke."

"You said freebasing. That's more than doing coke."

"Yes. Victor caught Natalie with ether. Ether can be used for freebasing. He and Sally threatened her with detox, and haven't caught her since. That doesn't mean she hasn't been using."

"Why do you put up with this family? They sound like nothing but trouble."

"What I do for a living is avert or create trouble. I'm good at it. I took this job because of Victor. He's a good man." He sighed and corrected himself, "He *was* a good man. And I gave him my word I'd help him."

I thought, *God help me, I've met someone who cares about keeping his word. I thought such people had gone extinct with the passenger pigeons.*

"What else?" he asked.

"Where were they all last night? And we need to find out how things stand with the takeover."

"Let's go," he said.

"You have to return the Porsche. That can be our excuse to find Sally and talk to her. She can tell us how to get in touch with Natalie. Do you know how to reach Ellis?"

"Yes. Or I know where he lives. And we should talk to Chip Vronsich. Until last month he was the CFO."

"Why did he leave?"

"I'm not sure. He resigned suddenly after many years. Victor said it was a private matter."

I thought for a second. "What will you do once this is finished? Where will you go?"

"Frankly, Scarlett, I don't give a damn." He smiled the little smile.

I walked the dogs, took a shower, and dressed

in my tell-me-everything outfit: navy slacks and a red pullover and red leather zip-front jacket. Strangers walk up and talk to me when I wear that jacket. I ate a blueberry muffin with cream cheese and drank some Irish Breakfast tea and went down to the garage.

Thorne was leaning into the Porsche, wiping down the driver's seat with damp paper towels; they came away brown with his dried blood. When he finished, he bent himself gingerly into the passenger seat without groaning or bleeding. Apparently I was the designated driver.

I backed out of the garage, avoiding any damage to my stucco or the neighbor's SUV, and I aimed the Porsche toward the ritziest street address in Pacific Heights, to the mansion where Victor Avery had lived until eleven o'clock last night.

≈𝒐≈

When we turned into the loop that is Presidio Terrace it was cold and the fog was starting to thin out for the day. The fire trucks were gone and so were the police cars and news vans that had jammed the street the night before. No doubt they were shooed away promptly by the senators and titans of commerce whose sleep they had disturbed.

We pulled up to a wrought-iron gate crossing the Avery's driveway and Thorne told me the numeric code to enter on the security keypad. The gate rolled open and we drove into the d-shaped cobblestone driveway of the cream-colored mansion.

This wasn't a new home. There was no outsized three-story portico blaring that here dwelt the neighborhood's parvenus. The mansion looked to be eighty or more years old, with tall, carefully trimmed juniper and camellia bushes flanking the recessed front door. No silver Jag was in sight.

What marred the mansion's tasteful understatement and guarded privacy were the shattered windows and smoke-blackened stucco at the front left corner of the house. Shrubbery was trampled and the driveway's pavers were dirty with soot and wet debris.

Tan plywood leaned against the house ready to be hammered over the gaping window frames. Two men working out of the back of a large white pickup truck were lifting the boards into place.

The cobblestone pavers continued along the side of the house down a slope to where I guessed there would be a rear garage. Thorne pointed there, and I drove the Porsche down past a three-door garage and parked the car against a retaining wall.

We uncurled out of the car and Thorne led the way up wide flagstone steps that curved around to a glass-paned door at the rear of the house. He held out his hand for his keys, then opened the door into a service porch connecting to a hallway. Pulling open a cupboard, he entered the alarm code and a flashing red light on the panel shifted to solid green.

The air in the house was thick with the smell of the fire, even though all the windows were wide open and a breeze was blowing through.

Someone was going to have to wash every fabric and swab every surface to get rid of the smell.

"Let's find Sally, if she's here," he said. We went walking slowly through the downstairs rooms. To the left was a twenty-five by forty-foot kitchen, fitted out with restaurant-grade stainless steel appliances, double dishwashers, and a big granite-topped island. The ceiling was at least nine feet high, with intricate crown molding.

Off the kitchen was a butler's pantry, a breakfast room with windows facing the garden, and a maid's room.

"Lupita the housekeeper might be here, or else she's shopping," Thorne said.

"I vote for she's got the day off," I said. "I think if the housekeeper were here the kitchen would show it."

We pushed through a swinging door from the kitchen into the formal dining room. On the wall was waist-high mahogany wainscoting and there were plum and grey-green fabrics on the elegant curtains and dining chairs. The high ceiling was coved. At the far end of the room the graceful downward curve in the ceiling plaster joined a curtained bay window.

A round, pedestal dining table was set for six and there was space to add multiple leaves. White tulips in a crystal vase on the sideboard drooped toward the polished wood surface and dropped their petals in sad disarray. There were paintings, still lifes, on the walls. I thought the modern one was a Van Hook, but the light in the dining room was dim and I made myself look away and follow Thorne out into the hall.

Across the marble-floored entry was the living room, stretching from the front to the back of the house, and out the tall rear windows was a view across the flower-filled garden to the Richmond District and on toward Lincoln Park and the Golden Gate.

In San Francisco people pay for views and land and reliably good weather, in that order. The Avery mansion had views and land; nobody gets reliably good weather in San Francisco, no matter what they pay.

The antique-filled living room was sodden, and the furniture looked like it wasn't in the correct places. Demi-lune tables stood away from the wall, a Waterford vase full of blush-colored peonies had fallen to the stained carpet and the artwork hung askew.

Chaotic this morning, the room was still as refined as everything else I'd seen in the house so far. It too had high ceilings, with in this room intricate dentile crown molding, embroidered carpets, and what looked like Brunschwig & Fils fabrics upholstering the couches and *bergère* chairs.

I walked in, my shoes sinking into the soaked rug, drawn to look at the Miro lithograph and— my God, a Pissarro landscape. Not a print, not a *giclée*. I stood there in front of the landscape staring, transported and no doubt betraying by my goony-eyed expression what a Pissarro freak I am. I had been to the Père Lachaise cemetery and planted flowers in Camille Pissarro's neglected grave, for heaven's sake.

"Xana?" Thorne asked. I heard him, but I didn't move. I might have been crying a little.

"Here we go," he said, putting his arm around my shoulders and shifting me toward the broken door of what Thorne had called the library. In a regular-size house you'd call it a den or a study, or, if you're using more recent terminology, a man-room.

Forced to look away from the painting, I saw there was yellow police tape across the door. I wiped my hands across my cheeks.

"The explosion," he said.

The destroyed library was what I had seen briefly in my mind's eye the previous night. Now, instead of fire and blood there was water and soot and a choking reek. I held my nose and breathed through my mouth.

There were dripping piles of leather- and hardbound books fallen open and jumbled on the floor. A flat-screen television mounted above the fireplace was cracked across the middle and the painting that slid down to cover it was fractured across the canvas and frame. I gasped at the damage to it. The colors in the landscape were vivid and it was new, not old. Maybe Francisco Moya. It could be restored.

A wide mahogany partner desk sat to the

right. Two dark green tufted leather wing chairs had blown over toward the desk and were leaning against it. From the direction things had blown down in, the explosion had originated in the center of the room, near the fireplace. A wall of bookshelves stretched to my left, and soggy, tattered books lay open like fallen birds on the carpet.

A cold early-morning wind blew through the windows and I was glad Thorne had his warm arm around me. A French door leading to the backyard had already been boarded up. As we stood staring at the wrecked library, the workmen hammered a piece of plywood into place over the last open window and the room was suddenly dark.

I had spent much of the previous year fixing up and redecorating my home, making it as beautiful as I could. My efforts were crap compared to the knowledge and skill that had filled this house with such exquisite things.

All these furnishings, the books and furniture and rugs and fabrics and paintings, had been made by artists who knew that their love for their craft would shine out of their work and endure through everything except, of course, fire and the flood that extinguishes a fire.

"Why aren't there any police or arson inspectors here?" I asked. "I thought there'd be crime scene people, insurance adjustors, somebody..."

"What if nobody thinks there was a crime?"

"Let's see if Mrs. Avery is upstairs," I said. In front of me was a horror which the pursuit of money may have caused but an ocean of money could not remedy. How could anyone come to terms with something like this?

Years ago, after some bad experience I was moaning about, my father had said to me, "Alexandra, life kills everybody, and there are attempted murders all along the way. Our job is to triumph over the ongoing mayhem." In other words, welcome to adulthood, and please get on with it. He had said this while hugging me, muting the awful truth of it and letting me know he sympathized with me in my current plight. I will not forget that moment with him; it was neither the first nor the last time he spoke to me in a kind-cruel fashion when I was behaving childishly, complaining, or refusing to accept responsibility for my own life and how I lived it.

I had learned from him, as we all do sooner or later, that somehow we must cope with the horrors life so haphazardly deals out. Even so, my heart went out to Mrs. Avery, since it seemed there was no friend here to watch over her, sit with her, listen to her, give her tissues when she wept, hold her hand, bring her tea. I didn't notice any pricey interior decorators showing up with casseroles.

Well, I was a stranger to her, but I was here and I would be a friend, if she would allow it.

Upstairs Thorne led me to an open door. Inside was a sitting room and beyond that a master bedroom. Here was the same expansive size and height, the same expensive, subtle style.

The furniture in the sitting room was covered in pale green and cream, with more wilted tulips on the secretary and on a chin-high painted Chinese armoire. It smelled of smoke up here too, but less so than downstairs, and the windows were open in a vain effort to clear out the smell.

Sitting sideways on the end of a chaise longue and facing the west window was the blonde woman I'd seen a fleeting image of in my mind's eye last night. I couldn't see her face but I was convinced it was her. Against the chilly breeze from the window she had wrapped a pale green cashmere throw around her like a shawl.

Slender, underneath the shawl she was wearing an untucked peacock blue silk T-shirt and close-fitting slacks the same color. An elegantly embroidered jacket had been thrown across the far side of the chaise. She wore embroidered Persian slippers on her feet. Her hair was shoulder-length, precisely cut and a glossy pale gold color only rich women seem able to acquire, but her hair hadn't been washed or combed this morning.

"Mrs. Avery?" Thorne said.

She turned. "Thorne?" she asked, getting up quickly from the chaise. "Where have you been?"

She saw me standing behind him and looked at him. "Oh, Thorne," she said again, dropping her shoulders. She was wearing makeup that was tired out, and it could not conceal dark circles under her vivid blue-green eyes. There were spots of black mascara flecking her upper and lower eyelids.

"This is Xana Bard, Mrs. Avery," he said.

"Where have you been? Have you heard about Victor?"

She ignored me. Her voice was soft and carefully modulated, perhaps a little practiced, a little artificial. I could see a box of tissues next to where she had been sitting, and a clump of crumpled tissues next to it.

"I was here," he answered. "We need to talk."

"They think it was an accident. They're telling me Victor killed himself by accident."

She looked unconvinced. She looked vacant and tentative and in pain as she hugged the cashmere to herself.

In spite of her fatigue and bedraggled grooming, I could see she had clear, fine-pored skin. She also radiated a sensuality that seemed completely unconscious. She was a woman men would gravitate to because it was her essential nature to love men, love sex, and love being loved.

In the way we all do, I drew immediate conclusions about someone I'd just met. Hers wasn't a classy nature, necessarily, but it wasn't calculating either. She was comfortable with who she was, and she took good care of herself, wearing clothes that clung to a body that even under the shawl was unmistakably lush. She didn't pretend she was anything more or less than herself, but then she didn't have to. She was a knockout, and no woman who looked like she did could avoid knowing it.

"Were you here?" Thorne asked her. "I saw the Jag leave, but I lost it." I let him do the talking; he didn't mention being shot.

"I was having dinner with friends at the Clift. I hired a driver to take me because I wanted to have some wine. If someone drove my car I don't know who it might have been."

"Is it in the garage?" he asked.

"I don't know," she said, more a question than an answer. Her tone said she hadn't thought there was any reason the Jaguar wouldn't be in the garage. She looked bewildered.

"Mrs. Avery," I said, stepping out from be-hind Thorne, "why don't you sit down and I'll get you something. Would you like some coffee or tea, or something stronger? You can't have had any sleep, and perhaps you'll allow me to take care of you a little. Would that be all right?"

"Lupita will be here," she said. I took it to mean "I'm declining politely because that's what one does under these circumstances."

"When will that be, do you know?"

"Tomorrow. I called and asked her to stay home today. I couldn't face trying to clean up." She looked apologetic about it.

"Of course not." I picked up an upholstered wastebasket and brushed the crumpled tissues into it. "Should I call a friend for you? Or some-one from your family?"

"No. I've already called my parents," she said.

"Do you know if there's tea? Or would you rather have some coffee? Or maybe you'd like to rest and I'll bring a coverlet for you."

"I'd love some black coffee," she said, as if she were wondering why she had forgotten how good coffee would taste.

She sat down and lifted her legs onto the chaise and looked at me, apparently deciding that my intent was kind. Perhaps she figured I was with Thorne and he trusted me, so maybe she'd give me the benefit of the doubt.

"Thank you," she said, and closed her eyes.

She settled herself against the backrest.

"I'll only be a minute," I said, grabbing from the bed and spreading a rose-colored mohair afghan over her legs. Thorne and I walked downstairs.

"I'm going to change, check the videos, and get Ellis's phone number," he said, heading toward a door at the end of the hall. He opened it and I saw stairs leading down to the garage.

I went into the kitchen and opened cabinets and the Sub-Zero until I found coffee and cups and filters for the coffeemaker.

Back upstairs I handed a cup of steaming coffee to Mrs. Avery. She smiled her thanks at me and held the rim of the cup to her lips without drinking. She took a deep breath, inhaling the aroma and letting it out slowly.

"Is it all right if I go into your bathroom?" I asked. "I'd like to bring you a damp facecloth."

She nodded and I walked into the master bedroom. Silver-framed photographs of her with Victor were spread across the wide dresser. In the pictures he was half a foot taller than she was, and his black hair and deep brown eyes were striking. She was photogenic, and her opposite coloring made her appear intensely feminine standing next to him. In the pictures they were usually laughing at the camera.

There were photos with daughter Natalie as well. Her face and figure were her mother's, but her hair and eyes were dark like Victor's. I imagined that no one meeting the family would guess she had been adopted.

"It's on the right," Sally called to me, and I opened the door into a Roman bath, with black and white marble floors, a soaking tub with jets, a steam shower with a tiled bench, a sauna, a privacy door for the water closet, and fluffy white sheepskin rugs in front of the twin sinks.

I found a thick terry washcloth folded in a drawer, soaked it in warm water, wrung it out and carried it to Mrs. Avery in my closed fist so it would hold its heat. She had the coffee cup up to her face, but it didn't look as if she'd drunk any.

"Here," I said, holding out my hand for the cup and handing her the warm terrycloth. "You have mascara on your face, and washing off makeup after a long night always makes me feel better."

She wiped at her eyes and cheeks and the washcloth turned black and flesh-toned with her makeup. When she was finished I took the cloth and asked her where her moisturizer was. It was La Mer of course, and I brought it to her after rinsing out the washcloth. She rubbed a little moisturizer on her face and neck and except for the shadows that darkened her undereyes, her translucent skin was recovered. I handed her the coffee.

"Can you drink any of it?" I asked her.

"I don't think so," she said. "But I like the smell. Thank you for making it."

"Shall I get you something to eat? Some toast, maybe?"

"I couldn't eat anything right now."

She seemed remarkably incurious about why I was there. She seemed disconnected from her surroundings, but then she had every right to be in shock. She spoke in a collected, quiet way, a little slowly so that it sounded almost as if she thought of each word individually before saying it.

I sat on the cushioned bamboo chair in front of the secretary. "Would you like to talk about what happened?" I asked.

"I don't know," she said after a pause. "I had to explain where I was to the police when I got home, and they asked me questions about the explosion, but I was out last night. I didn't know anything. They said it looked like an accident and left. They put the tape across the door and said to stay out of the library in case they needed to come back for anything."

Her hands began to tremble. I reached for the coffee cup and she handed it to me.

"Why don't you tell me as much or as little as you feel like about your husband? Where you met, what he was like, what you both liked to do, all that. Only if you want to. Thorne says Victor was a very good man," I started for her.

"Oh, he was. He was very good to me. He was good to everyone. At least he tried to be."

"How did you meet?"

She reached for a tissue and curled her hand

around it, ready in case she began to cry. She thought for a moment before beginning the story.

"I was catering a Young Presidents event in Princeton. He came looking for me to tell me how much he liked the food. Nobody ever did that unless they were hitting on me, so I ignored him."

"And then what?"

"He kept talking to me. I was working, you know? Replenishing trays and telling the staff what to do, but he kept asking me questions and flattering me. He was nice enough but it was a little aggravating."

I could hear the undertone of an East Coast accent creeping into her voice. She was relaxing as she talked, and she'd had no sleep, and her controlled speech was slipping into something less conscious. Her voice was less airy and soft; it was thinner and higher.

"Are you from back east?" I asked.

"Yes. From Trenton. It's pretty rough now, but when I grew up there were still decent neighborhoods. My dad owned a restaurant. Savio's. It wasn't fancy, but there were a lot of regulars."

"I thought maybe you had met Mr. Avery in college."

"I didn't go to college. I was working in the restaurant after high school and I got knocked up." This was definitely a Jersey girl talking now.

"I needed a lot of babysitting from my Aunt Gianetta before I had my catering business up and running. I worked my ass off to get gigs like the Young Presidents meeting. It was guys flattering me, telling me I was gorgeous, that got me in trouble when I was seventeen, so I didn't encourage Victor." She laughed ruefully and looked at me. "But there was no shutting him down, thank God."

"What did he do?"

"He took my business card and said he'd be staying in the area for a couple of days. He said he had clients that he had to call on, but he would make time for me. I think he said the DuPonts were customers. I figured he was blowing smoke. He wasn't wearing a wedding ring, but a lot of married guys took them off when they tried to pick me up."

"But you agreed to see him."

"Yeah. I hadn't gone on a date in three years. He came to the house and handed me flowers. Tulips. Nobody'd ever bought me flowers before. And my dad never bought tulips for the restaurant. He said they wilted too fast; they weren't worth the money. He always bought daisies and mums, and changed the water every day so he could get every last nickel's worth out of 'em." She was staring ahead of her, seeing her younger self in the shabby restaurant with the cheap flowers.

"I remember Victor came to the door wearing the nicest suit. He looked so distinguished. It was dark gray and fit him like it was made for him. I found out later that all his suits were made for him, but in those days I couldn't imagine any such a thing. My aunt flipped for him, but my pop told me to watch out."

"Where did Victor take you?"

"To a really swanky place outside Philadelphia. The Waverly Grill, I think it was. We started talking in the car and kept talking all through dinner and all the way home. He was so easy to talk to. He told me he admired me for getting the catering business up on its feet all by myself. He told me about his father leaving him the chemical business and I realized he really did have the DuPonts for customers. But even with all his money, he felt like an old friend right from the start."

She looked very wistful. Her eyes were brimming and I handed her a tissue; she'd forgotten the one in her hand.

"It sounds like you made a good pair. I was looking at the photographs on your dresser and they all seem to show you laughing together."

"We did laugh," she said, pressing the tissues to her eyes. "We've been very happy."

She had slender, graceful fingers with carefully manicured nails. A two-carat diamond flashed on her ring finger next to a platinum wedding band with pavé diamonds. It was a rock, all right, but it sat low in the setting and was splendid rather than gaudy.

She put down her hands and looked at me.

"He never made me feel like anything but a

lady. I wasn't a lady, but Victor treated me like one so I made it my business to be one for him. And he was wonderful to Natalie. He adopted her and sent her to the best schools. He gave her a lot of love. He just—he deserved nothing but happiness and I did everything I could to give it to him." She pressed the tissues to her eyes.

"He sounds like a sweetheart. And it sounds like he adored you."

She sat, not speaking, and her breath came out in a little shuddering sob.

"Tell me about your daughter. Is she home?"

Down went the tissues and she looked straight at me, the tears dried in her bloodshot eyes. "She's not here right now."

"Does she know about her dad?"

"Yes. I spoke to her last night. She's staying with a friend." She was staring at me and her pronunciation was abruptly careful and clipped.

"Where is she? Can I help in some way?"

"No, thank you. You've been very kind."

Back again was the cultivated speech I'd heard earlier. Her voice had changed as well; it was softer and full of air, reclaimed from the hard edge she'd drifted into unwittingly. A conversational door was slamming shut. I gave it one more try.

"It sounds like something is troubling you in some way. I know it's none of my business, and you don't have to tell me about it. I have a feeling everything is not as it should be. Sometimes it helps to say things out loud in order to figure them out."

She gave me the look of someone assessing her choices, and then she made one.

"Natalie's in rehab," she said.

"Ahhh." I spread the sound out and nodded, as if the information made sense.

"For how long?" I asked.

"She went in this past weekend," Sally replied. Today was Monday.

"She was using drugs and cutting classes and we had had words about it. Victor and I decided there was no other choice."

"Where is she?"

"At Mountain Top Retreat."

Sally had named the place people send drugged-out addicts or DT-level drunks to, but only if the family is rich and the addict is completely out of control. It's a last resort, for when families want their dear ones locked up and prevented from selling off any more jewelry or electronics or bearer bonds.

The facility provides thorough and reputable detox programs and counseling; nevertheless it's jail, but with better sheets.

If Sally was at a dinner party last night and Natalie was behind bars up in Marin County, who was driving the Jaguar and shooting at Thorne?

Sally's glance shifted to the bedroom doorway and I turned to see Thorne standing there in a clean cotton shirt and pants. The shirt had pale green and yellow stripes on oxford cloth, and he had buttoned his cuffs. The pants were dark green denim. He had shaved and his hair was wet, and he looked like a very large forest-dwelling creature, or maybe Robin Hood via Andover. I worried about how he had showered without getting the wound and bandages wet, but kept mum in front of Sally.

"The Jaguar is in the garage," he said.

"Are you sure it was my car you saw last night?" Sally asked.

"It was AVERY4," he said, and I guessed all the family car license plates were personalized.

"Oh," she said. "Well that's strange." She thought about it for a minute.

"Thorne," she went on, changing the subject, "I know your arrangement was with Victor, but I'd like to know if you would remain here for at least a little while. I would be grateful for your help with some of the things that will be necessary. Dealing with the funeral and the lawyers and the chemical business, and the takeover attempt from Ellis."

She took a deep breath and looked out the window. "You were once a part of that upper-crust realm and I never was. I know I'll need advice on how to sort through all that."

"Okay," he said. "But I'll need to be gone sometimes. I have to find out who did this."

She continued to stare out the window, taking

in what Thorne had just said. She inhaled as if she was about to say something, but then she seemed to change her mind.

She turned to Thorne and said, "I'll give you Victor's cell phone, if that's all right with you. That way I can reach you and vice versa if something comes up."

"Who is the police officer handling this?" I asked.

"I can't remember. Jackson? Johnson? He gave me a card, of all things. It's downstairs in the front hall. I never imagined policemen would have business cards."

She'd learned how to mimic a lady all right. I could imagine my mother saying something that smacked just as thoroughly of *noblesse oblige*.

"Could you find out what happens next?" Sally said, speaking to Thorne. "The officer said there would have to be an autopsy before there could be a funeral."

"I'll call him."

"I have to talk to James Petersen today. He's Victor's attorney and there must be documents I have to see or do something about..."

Staring into the carpet, she was probably realizing the documents would include Victor's will and any trusts he or his father had set up. Victor was dead, and she would have to manage the estate and Victor's unstable business affairs, plus this house and any other homes they owned around the world. It was a lot to take in. There would be a great deal for her to do besides bury her husband and grieve.

"Should I call Peterson?" Thorne asked.

"No, thank you. I'd better be the one to do that," she said.

"What else needs to be done to secure the house? The library windows are boarded up."

"Oh, thank God. The firemen helped me find a twenty-four-hour service and the men got here within a couple of hours or I don't know what I would have done. Having those windows blown out, having the house wide open like that, it was frightening."

"Mrs. Avery," I said, "is there anything else you need right now? I'd be happy to stay with you if you like..."

"No, I'm fine now. You've been extremely kind, but I'd rather be on my own." Her voice held a new air of authority.

Turning to Thorne, she told him she would get Victor's phone for him and walked out of the bedroom and down the hall.

"You don't have your own cell phone?" I asked him.

"No," was all he said. I guess it was part of the off-the-grid strategy.

Thorne and I walked out into the hall, and Sally came out of another bedroom holding an iPhone and a charger cord. Thorne took them and slid them into his pants pocket.

"Please excuse me for not seeing you out," she

said. "I don't want to go down there yet." The look she gave us seemed to say she might never want to go downstairs again.

We said good bye and she turned back to her chilly boudoir.

≍8≍

Thorne and I walked downstairs and out to the Porsche. He drove this time, down Divisadero to Market Street.

He was utterly competent behind the wheel. In fact, Thorne seemed utterly competent all around, except for the part about being an invisible man with a bullet wound, but even that seemed a form of rare and admirable capability.

I found myself relaxing into the amicable silence between us. He answered only the question you asked him, and that briefly, but he wasn't pinched or worried or troubled. He was comfortably settled inside his skin.

I generally have to quell my nervousness when I'm a passenger, forcing my arm onto the armrest instead of gripping the Hail Mary handle over the door with both hands. I prefer to be the driver so I can remain vigilant at all times.

San Francisco drivers consist mostly of Caucasians and African-Americans from some state other than California, Hispanics from all over Central and South America, Pacific Islanders, and Asians from China to Cambodia to Japan and the Philippines. Plus tourists from everywhere.

What that results in is no consistent driving style except unsignaled last-minute turns from the wrong lane, multiplied by speed and discourtesy. We kill off a goodly number of pedestrians and cyclists annually, ramming into them as we run red lights, and for some reason they neglect to mention these homicides in the tourist brochures for "Everybody's Favorite City."

With Thorne I left my arms in my lap and turned away from the windshield to talk with him. "You're a very good driver," I told him.

"Thanks," he said. "You too."

I smiled. "What's the difference between a regular Nine-Eleven and the C4S?" I asked.

"Really?"

"Not really. I thought you might want to explain it to me. In my experience, guys who own cars like this tend to want to talk about them."

"I don't own it." He was amused, the little smile indicated.

"By the way," he went on, "no surveillance video."

"The cameras didn't work?"

"Video was removed."

"And you didn't hear anybody come in to the house last night?"

"No. The security equipment is in the garage. The living room door to the library is soundproofed. There's a door to the outside from the library."

"So it's a dead end, except that whoever was there last night knew about the video and the outside door."

"Correct." We swerved smoothly around the S-curve that converted Divisadero into Castro Street.

"Didn't you go down to the garage to get this car?"

"Yes, but not until I'd gone to the library and seen—the damage. You can get into the garage from outside using a keypad."

"And the Jaguar drove away with the video," I said.

"Check," he said. We were amicably silent again.

"A personal question?" he said.

"Yes, since you have such lovely if taciturn manners. I might not answer, but shoot."

"Your first name," he said, with no interrogatory inflection.

It wasn't exactly a surprise, this non-question question. I'd heard it in one form or another for as long as I'd sported the name.

"My little sister couldn't pronounce 'Alexandra,' but she could manage 'Ex-Anna,' and every-body in my family started calling me that. At first they did it to tease me and I didn't like it very much. But when I got to prep school I thought it was normal to have a nickname and nice not to have Buffy-Cuffy-Muffy-Tuffy like all the other WASP girls..."

"Do people mangle it?"

"Pretty often, but I just pronounce it once and forget about it. I'll answer to Zana or Ex-Anna, either way. My friends mostly say it right, but even mispronounced it's better than telling peo-ple I'm Alexandra because then they shorten it to Alex, and I don't care for that at all, thank you very much, and no, I don't have any good reason why that is the case, but it is.

"Anyway, the Averys," I went on. "Sally wouldn't talk about Natalie other than to say that she was in rehab," I told him.

"As of when?" he asked.

"As of this weekend. She's supposed to be at Mountain Top Retreat."

"Probably for the best," he said.

"Could she have come home last night to see Victor?"

"Maybe," he said.

"What I've heard about that place, once you're in, you're in until whoever locked you up lets you out."

"Might be a good idea with Natalie."

"Did you see Natalie this weekend?"

"No," he said. "Victor and I were at a charity golf tournament in Monterey until last night."

"Sally went to another room to get Victor's cell phone. Did they share a bedroom or did they each have their own?" Having dual master suites was always in vogue with the wealthy, but I asked because I was nosy.

"They each had a bedroom."

"Did they seem as happy together as she told me they were?"

"She lit him up. He was very proud of her, never embarrassed about showing it."

"What about her?"

He thought about it. "She deferred to him. She dressed up every day, fixed his breakfast, poured his coffee. As if her job was to look great so he could stay proud."

He thought some more. "I heard them arguing only once, about Natalie. I never saw her take advantage. He was uxorious, yes. Dominated, no."

I hadn't heard the word 'uxorious' since I took five years of Latin in prep school. Uxor translates to wife, so my recollection was that it meant somebody who doted on his wife.

We were winding around the curves of upper Market Street, along the corniche on the edge of the Twin Peaks hillside. Glimpsed between houses, the view of the San Francisco Bay is breathtaking, when the fog clears and you can see it. You couldn't see the view this morning, just murk.

"Did Victor own a gun?" I asked.

"Yes. A Glock, unloaded, locked in the library safe."

"I wonder if it's still there."

"I don't know the combination," he said.

"Sally was telling me about how she and Victor met. I could hear her New Jersey upbringing come out in her speech as she talked about it. When I asked her about Natalie she snapped into her 'Mrs. Victor Avery' voice. I have this feeling she was hiding more than a mother would cover up, just to keep the family secrets from a stranger. What else do you know about either Sally or Natalie?"

"When Victor brought Natalie home she was okay for a while, but this past semester she began acting up again. She and Sally could get loud."

"Did Victor ever remark on it?"

"No. But she used to be his little princess, and now she was sullen with him. He told me it was a phase."

"He and Sally knew about the drugs?" I asked.

"Yes."

"I can guess that was a shock to both of them. I guess drugs always are, even though nowadays anytime you raise kids who aren't pregnant and smoking crack in prison by the time they turn twelve it seems like a miracle."

Thorne smiled his infinitesimal smile.

"Could it have had anything to do with Ellis

showing up? Didn't he show up about the same time she started acting out again?" I said.

"Yes, but Ellis was never in the house. Victor only met him in restaurants or hotels, and never with Sally and Natalie. Once Ellis made his move to take over the company, Victor didn't talk to him again."

"Tell me about Ellis."

"I don't like him." He said it plainly, without any emphasis. "The veneer of success seems thin. Sally was uneasy about him."

"How so?"

"Victor said he tried to talk to Sally about Ellis, but when he brought up the subject she got defensive, like he was accusing her of something."

Why was the Avery Chemical takeover the only taboo topic between Victor and Sally? Why had Natalie's seemingly recovered life gone off the rails again at about the time Ellis showed up?

Thorne continued winding up Market Street and in amicable silence we drove uphill to find Victor's no-longer-employed Chief Financial Officer.

≈*9*≈

The Upper Market neighborhood is a mix of gay and straight, but mostly gay, renters and owners. The houses clinging to the edge of the Twin Peaks hill on the Bay side are small and stucco-clad. The apartment buildings tucked tightly against the uphill slope have in many cases been converted to condos.

House or condo, the homes have a one hundred eighty-degree view of downtown and the San Francisco Bay, from Candlestick Point to the Golden Gate; at least they do whenever the fog isn't in. The fog was still in.

San Francisco neighborhoods change names and character every six or eight blocks. Each neighborhood has its own little shopping district, its own style and demographics.

Wherever you live, it's usually only a block or two at most to get to a mom and pop grocery store, a dry cleaners, a florist, a coffee place, and at least a half dozen restaurants, all of which serve very good food at reasonable prices.

Except for the downtown financial district and the Fisherman's Wharf tourist ghetto, the City is an assemblage of fifty or so of these pint-sized villages. Because public transportation is everywhere and most residents can walk to the stores and services they need, it's possible to live here and get around the City without owning a car. It's possible, but everybody owns a car anyway, and can never find anywhere to park it.

Thorne pressed the doorbell to 156 Portola, a flat-faced, 60's-era four-story multi-condo building, and we waited. After thirty seconds or so, he rang the bell again. We waited some more. I was wondering why we were being so patient but as usual Thorne gave the impression that he knew exactly what he was doing. He rang the bell a third time.

"Who is it?" came a scratchy tenor voice from the speaker next to the bell.

"Thorne."

The buzzer sounded and the door clicked. Thorne held it open for me to go in ahead of him. Inside, the lobby wall was lined with floor-to-ceiling mirrors reflecting a row of ficus trees in matching glazed pots along the opposite wall. In front of the trees there were dark green marble benches sitting on the polished black marble floor. Our footsteps echoed as we approached the elevator.

On the top floor we turned toward an open door at the end of the hall. Light flooded toward us from the apartment's huge plate glass windows.

Standing in the doorway, a silhouetted Chip Vronsich was barefoot, wearing a belted terry-cloth robe with a Ralph Lauren logo on the chest pocket. He looked to be in his mid-forties, and he looked exhausted. It was nine-thirty in the morning, and he yawned and rubbed his eyes.

"Hello dreamboat," he said to Thorne, clasping Thorne's huge hand with both of his own. "Who's your lovely lady friend in the fabulous jacket?"

"Chip, I'd like you to meet Xana Bard." Chip and I shook hands and said hello, and he stepped back and waved for us to come inside. "Give me a minute, will you? Please, make yourselves at home."

He disappeared into a room down the hall and shut the door. I looked at the living room in front of me, full of chrome and taupe leather and black suede, fastidiously kept. There were no curtains on the windows, but I could see a rolled-up scrim across the top that would drop down over the glass to kill the sun's glare if and when the fog cleared and the stunning view emerged.

To the left was a dining area with a glass-topped table and armless, black silk-draped chairs. The kitchen was small, industrial chic, with solid copper countertops and a bar with three chrome and black leather stools on the living room side.

There were big unframed black and white photographs on the living room wall: nude men folding their bodies into shapes that emphasized form and curvature and shadows rather than anatomy.

Chip returned wearing black jeans, black loafers with no socks, and a thin, violet cotton V-neck sweater. He had pushed the sleeves up his arms and was combing his fingers through his thick brown hair to push it off his forehead. He hadn't shaved; his trim mustache was surrounded by gaunt, unshaven cheeks that glinted with gray hairs among the brunette shadow. A gold ID bracelet flashed on his wrist. In his clothes instead of the bulky robe he was whippet thin, and with the light from the windows shining on his face instead of backlighting him I could see the striking pallor of his face and neck.

"Would you like some coffee? I'm going to make some," he said, walking into the kitchen and reaching for the cupboard doors.

"Sure," said Thorne.

"Me too," I said. I don't particularly like coffee, but when someone offers hospitality I believe you should accept it without quibbling; after all, nobody's going to pry your jaws open and force the coffee down your throat through a funnel. We sat on barstools and watched Chip pull a bag of whole beans out of the freezer and grind them.

"So what brings you to see me?" he asked Thorne once the coffee was dripping and he had placed mugs, spoons, napkins, a milk pitcher and a sugar bowl in front of us. "Luke, have you decided to come over to the dark side?" he said in a deep voice, batting his eyelashes.

Chip was leaning forward across the countertop, brown eyes gazing at Thorne and his hands palm down on either side of him. Such provocative behavior would make your average straight guy squirm and then either slug somebody or make an abrupt dash for the exit, but Thorne seemed used to it. Or maybe Thorne was gay. He had acknowledged that women flirted with him; he hadn't mentioned whether he flirted with them as well. But Chip's question seemed to indicate that Thorne was straight. Not that I cared. But then why was I wondering about it? Because people wonder about such things, that's why.

Something was wrong with how Chip looked, as I watched him. Now and again I could see his eyes rolling upward and his eyelids sliding closed, and then they would slide back open and he would focus again.

"You haven't heard about Victor," Thorne said.

"Oh no," said Chip, rearing back, vamping no longer. "Did that little turd Ellis manage to steal the company?"

"Chip, Victor was killed last night, at the house."

"Oh Jesus." He put his hands to his face. "Oh Jesus God." He looked back at Thorne. "Did they catch anybody? Was it Ellis?"

"The police told Sally it was an accident."

"Do *you* believe that? I don't believe that." Chip shook his head from side to side. "Poor Victor."

The coffeemaker gurgled that it was finished brewing and Chip reached for the pot. He poured for us all.

"Chip," Thorne said, "I have to find out why Victor was killed."

"Of course, of course. Oh God, this is *terrible*." He was looking down at the floor and shaking his head, holding his hand to his forehead. I thought he might be working his way up to tears.

"Do you mind telling us why you left the company?" I said, stirring cream and sugar into my coffee.

"Who are you again? I'm sorry, I've forgotten your name already. This is such a shock," he said.

"My name is Xana Bard. I'm a friend of Thorne's, and we're looking into Victor's death because neither of us believes it was an accident."

"Why not?" he asked, looking at each of us in turn. He was all business now, cautious, professional, analyzing the situation and deciding how much of what he knew he should reveal to us.

"I was at the house," Thorne said. "I drove after them and someone shot me."

"You were shot?" Chip was startled. "How badly? Are you all right? Why aren't you in the hospital?" The words flew out of him in a rush.

"I'm fine."

"Jesus. I know you're a real man and all, but I don't know anybody else who'd be up and around after something like that. Are you sure you're okay?"

"No, but there'll be time to sit around mending after I find out what happened to Victor."

"What do you want to know?" Chip asked.

"We're piecing together a timeline," I said, "trying to figure out how everything might have happened. We don't know what's relevant or not, so we're just asking all the people who knew Victor to tell us as much as they can.

"I realize this may be very personal," I went on, "but I'd appreciate it if you would tell us why you left Avery Chemical a month ago. Thorne tells me you'd worked with Victor for many years."

Chip was silent. We let him think about whether or not to tell us. It doesn't help to encourage someone verbally, so we encouraged him psychically. Well, I did anyway. Finally he sighed and said, "Victor asked me to leave and I knew he was right to ask, so I left."

"Why was he right to ask?" I said.

Chip sipped some coffee and thought about

his answer. "Because he knew I was having some problems." He stopped. He gazed out the window at the fog. Thorne and I waited in amicable silence.

"Chip," Thorne said finally.

"I know you won't blab," Chip said. "I just— it's very private."

I drank some coffee. It was exceptional coffee, if you like that sort of thing. We watched Chip wrestle with his qualms.

"It's such a fucking cliché," he laughed ruefully. "I'm gay, I live in San Francisco, so what do you expect? Six years ago I tested positive for HIV." Thorne and I said nothing. What can you say?

"I started taking the prescriptions, the 'cocktail' they call it for God's sake, like you're at some dressy party instead of hanging on for all you're worth to a life that can disintegrate into dozens of cancers and dementia and one loss of dignity after the other. So far I've had no symptoms. So far I'm wonderfully healthy," he laughed ruefully. "But after five years of living with the virus, not being able to stand the thought of infecting someone else, living on my own and knowing it was a matter of time until the virus got creative and outsmarted the drugs, something just snapped.

"No matter how trite my circumstances must seem to everybody else, living with HIV creates the most horrible isolation. People still have crazy prejudices about it, so I keep it quiet. I was an executive at a major manufacturing company. My boss was the owner and a socially prominent man whom I did not want to embarrass. I'd known Victor since right after I graduated from Wharton. I was closeted in those days, but he stuck by me even after I came out.

"So I kept a lid on all of it—the diagnosis, my fears, the vigilance I had to exert in order to take the pills every day at the exact same time, without anybody knowing why I walked out of meetings, or always had to have a bottle of water with me. God, the loneliness and the shame, you cannot imagine. I shut a lot of myself down in order to deal with it.

"But gay people more than most know there's a price you pay for suppressing who you are. I lost patience with the daily grind. I wanted more—more experiences, more life in whatever time I had left. I was jealous of everybody who wasn't living with a death sentence. I was something, anyway. Who knows what it was? I mean, I realize everybody lives with a death sentence. It's only in California and maybe Tibet that people imagine death might be optional. Somehow I convinced myself that my situation was worse than everybody else's." He thought about what he wanted to say next.

"And then it really was worse," he laughed. "Five months ago at a checkup I mentioned abdominal pain and some weight loss, and after the tests my doctor told me I had stage three pancreatic cancer. Given my HIV status, chemo and radiation were not advisable. Pancreatic cancer is very tough to beat, even with the most aggressive treatment. Untreated, well..."

"Jesus," Thorne said.

Chip nodded and grinned.

"Yessiree," he said. "Anyway, I'd always smoked some grass and done poppers and Ex, and when a friend offered me uppers, boom, down the hatch they went. And honeychild, it was heavenly." He looked at me and smiled ruefully; his eyes rolled shut and then opened again.

"I never had to sleep. Sleep was wasted time, since my days were numbered. I wanted to fill up every waking hour with more and more life. The rest is the same sad story it always is. I started making mistakes on the job, missing work because I forgot what day it was, not returning phone calls, blowing off meetings with analysts. It was unforgivable.

"Victor asked me about it, but I refused to admit anything was wrong. Last month Victor found me with my head down on my desk, crashed and unconscious. I'd missed an SEC filing.

"That morning there was an article in the business section of the *Chronicle* about problems between the Avery brothers. The reporter hinted that a takeover might be imminent because of financial negligence by the current executives. Victor couldn't let me off the hook any longer. I'd gone over the edge too publicly.

"Being Victor, he was genuinely sorry. He offered me paid rehab, counseling, medical coverage for another year, all paid for out of his own pocket. I was so cranked I nearly took him up on it, but I managed to resign without completely destroying my self-respect."

"And you're still addicted," I said.

"Absolutely. No rest for the weary, but then with meth you never feel weary," he said. "The good news is I really don't have that long to worry about it. Recovery programs take longer than I have left. The cancer is stage four now. That means I should get my affairs in order, as the saying goes. Forget about AIDS. Stage five means I'm in a body bag being carted out of my house by the coroner."

"I'm so sorry," I said. He reached over and patted my hand, as if I were the one who required comforting.

"Thanks," he said. We were all quiet for a few moments.

"Do you know what's happening with the company stock?" I asked him. "Thorne says Victor owned a majority."

"He does. He did. Somebody was selling to Ellis, though. A friend at the brokerage informed us that every share Ellis could lay his hands on, he was buying. I'm pretty sure the board members were selling because Ellis's purchases kept pushing the share price up. Even though the board members risk insider trading prosecution by the SEC, many of them had to have sold their shares for Ellis to acquire so much of the company. I don't know how he pulled it off. Maybe he had some dirt on them."

Chip was silent again. "He had dirt on me, after all."

"What?" Thorne and I both spoke at once.

"He knew I was HIV positive, and he knew I was a speed freak. I have no idea how he knew, but he knew. He told me to falsify the stock purchase records so his name wouldn't show up owning such a big percentage of the company. He wanted to blindside Victor and force the board to make him a member. I told him the CFO doesn't track stock purchases, that the brokerage handles stock sales and shareholder relations for us. He said I would have to find a way or he would tell Victor and the newspapers about me."

"When did he threaten you?"

"A week before Victor asked me to leave. That's why I fell apart and missed the SEC filing. I refused to help Ellis, but I spent the week more loaded than usual and I collapsed on my desk because I was so wrecked. And sure enough, there was the newspaper article the morning Victor found me. I'm sure that was Ellis's doing. It was actually a relief when Victor fired me. It meant Ellis couldn't threaten me with anything anymore, and maybe it would slow him down."

"Was any other big shareholder selling shares

to Ellis?"

"I have no idea."

We all took a sip of coffee.

"What do you know about Victor's daughter?" I asked.

"She ran away last year. Victor was worried sick about it. But he found her and she came home. That's all I know."

"So what are you going to do now?".

He thought for a few moments.

"I have no idea. I'm not sure how much longer I'll be on my feet."

Thorne and I looked at each other and back at Chip.

"Don't offer me any help, please," Chip said, shaking his head. "I don't deserve any help." He paused for a moment and went on.

"I loved and admired Victor Avery. He was the most honorable man, the most decent man, I have ever known. And I let him down. Badly. My parents are from Croatia. My mother used to say 'you buttered your bread, now you have to sleep in it.' I'm not sleeping very much these days, and when I do it's badly, but it's my bread and I have to figure out how to get it unbuttered. Or if that will even be possible, now that Victor is dead."

"You make delicious coffee," I said to say something, even an idiotic something, and stood up to go.

"It's a start," he smiled, escorting us to the door. He put his hand on my shoulder as we walked, more comfort for me, I thought.

He reached out to shake hands when we left. This time it was Chip's hand that disappeared into both of Thorne's.

≈**10**≈

As we walked to the car I couldn't bring myself to say anything about Chip. I'd already been facile and shallow, complimenting him on his coffee; I wanted to avoid doing any more of that.

"Where to next?" I asked Thorne as we climbed into the Porsche.

"Ellis Avery." He took Victor's iPhone and a slip of paper from his shirt pocket and pressed numbers on the screen. He held the phone up to his ear.

"Mr. Avery? This is Thorne Ardall. I worked for your brother... Yes, I'm sorry about the news as well... I wonder if I might see you for a few minutes... Today, if possible...   Thank you, I should be about twenty or thirty minutes."

"Well that was simple," I said.

"He sounded upset," Thorne said.

"If he's the villain in this piece, maybe he's acting."

"It didn't strike me as acting."

"Okay. Where does he live?"

"Woodside."

"Well, to the estate please, Jeeves."

Woodside is on the peninsula south of San Francisco, and is a sylvan suburban neighborhood, heavy on the "neigh." The horsey set lives there in homes with names rather than houses with addresses. Jacqueline Onassis once owned a place in Woodside, so you can imagine. What you see from the two-lane winding roads is white rail fences and gated driveways with name plaques for the houses rather than the owners; "Casa Feliz," that sort of thing.

Thorne drove. As he headed down Portola to Junipero Serra I pulled out my cell phone to check on whether Natalie was indeed in rehab.

"Mountain Top Retreat," a pleasant female voice answered.

"Hello. My name is Xana Bard and I'd like to speak with Natalie Avery, if I may."

"One moment please," she said, and there was a pause. She didn't put me on hold, and I could hear computer keys clicking.

"I'm sorry, Ms. Bard, we don't give out any information regarding our residents."

She hadn't actually answered my question, had she? I tried again. "Would it be possible for you to confirm whether or not Natalie is actually staying with you?"

"It would not be possible. We don't give out any information at all. I'm sure you understand."

"May I leave a message for her?"

"I'm afraid that won't be possible."

"Because she's not staying with you, or because residents are not allowed to receive messages?" I was speaking in my most pleasant tone, but even I was annoyed by me. Thorne made a little snorting sound that might have been a laugh.

"Thank you for calling. Have a nice day," she said, and hung up.

"They don't give out information about their residents," I told him. "There's no knowing whether she's there or not. I think they either looked her up on a patient list or else they looked me up to see if I'm authorized to talk to her. Either way, their lips are zipped."

We were on Highway 280 now, headed south down the Peninsula. As soon as we passed the turnoff to San Francisco Airport the fog evaporated, the sky cleared to brilliant blue, and the bright sun shone down upon us. We rolled quietly and smoothly to the Woodside exit and then up into the hills.

The first winter rains had brought a green blush to the cheeks of the bleached, grass-stubbled hillsides, and the tree branches were misty with pink and maroon leaf buds ready to burst into emerald.

Thorne turned into an open-gated driveway and drove upward around the edge of a hill to an angular wood and glass house. It was big but not monstrous, and sat in the middle of a eucalyptus grove.

The trees were shedding their gray bark in hanging strips, showing paler skin beneath. Their trunks look to me like someone is scraping off old wallpaper, and the fallen leaves and seed pods smell like cat piss. What eucalyptuses lack in visual and olfactory aesthetics they compensate for by having shallow roots that permit the top-heavy, iron-hard trees to fall over onto your roof in a strong wind, crushing you while you sleep. In this house, if the falling tree didn't kill you, the splintering glass shards would.

Ellis walked outside into the warm day before we had climbed out of the car, and waved us toward him. He looked like a thinner, shorter, meaner Victor, with a little less black hair on top and a little more in his scowling caterpillar eyebrows.

Even though Victor was the elder of the two, Ellis's face looked more weathered, creased with crow's-feet and marionette lines. His frown was thunderous and his manner was peremptory.

"What do you know about last night?" he demanded of Thorne.

"Mr. Avery, allow me to introduce Xana Bard," Thorne said.

"Hi." He nodded at me without making eye

contact. No handshake, no European-style dou-ble-cheek kiss. I was going to have to manage my temper in the face of this man's rudeness. I re-minded myself his brother had just died, and we were going to interrogate him just in case he was a murderer.

"How do you do?" I said.

Ignoring me, turning to Thorne, Ellis asked again, "What have you heard about the explo-sion?"

"Is there somewhere that we could talk?" Since Ellis was forgetting his manners, Thorne was coaching him; we were still standing on the flagstone entryway.

"Yes, yes, come in," Ellis said, pivoting and leading us inside.

The house was one huge room on the ground floor, with no interior walls to block the view of the coastal range outside the glass. I could see the shimmering steel-blue Pacific Ocean in the dis-tance. It felt like we were outside, even with the high roof over our heads.

"Please sit," he said curtly, and we followed him to two long benches padded in button-tufted navy leather. He waved to indicate where we should sit.

"Now," he said, seated and facing Thorne, "what happened?"

"May I please have a glass of water?" Thorne asked him. Ellis straightened up and looked at Thorne more carefully. He said, "Certainly," stood up and walked across the room.

I have seen my mother do this number on those she deems socially incompetent. They practically give extra-unit credit for this kind of irreproachable put-down at prep schools everywhere. Thorne had to be doing this consciously, Ellis had to know Thorne was doing it, and Ellis had to have been infuriated by it.

"Anything for you?" Ellis asked me from the kitchen as he reached for a glass. He was being a host, but his word choice and tone were clear; he was complying with the social code, but under protest.

"No, thank you."

He walked across the room and held out the glass. Thorne thanked him, took the glass, drank most of the contents and set it down gently on the hammered metal coffee table, but not before looking around to see if there was a coaster. There was no coaster. We all silently acknowledged the gaffe that the absence of a coaster represented.

Ellis, shamed by his unwelcome visitors, sat down and asked again with barely controlled irritation what had happened. Thorne, having successfully completed the shaming, told him about the explosion, leaving out the car chase and the shooting.

I sat up straight, crossed my legs at the ankles, tucked them under the bench, and held my hands quiet in my lap. I wondered if I would have an opportunity to remark politely on the weather. I did not hold out much hope of that.

"But how could the explosion have happened?" Ellis pressed Thorne. "Victor knew how to handle ether. It's toxic. It's dangerous. It's highly volatile and flammable. It's not something you'd keep in your house."

He was frustrated and angry, and he was leaning forward with his elbows on his knees and one hand cupping the side of his head. "It requires special refrigeration and containers. It couldn't have been suicide either. He'd never have misused ether that way."

"What do *you* think happened?" Thorne asked.

"I haven't the slightest idea," he said.

"Mr. Avery," I said, using my tea-party voice in response to Ellis's resentfulness, "I'd like to know what you plan to do, now that Victor no longer stands in the way of your acquisition of Avery Chemical."

"Who are you?" he glared at me.

"Xana is a friend, Mr. Avery," Thorne explained. "She's helping me."

"Are you with the papers?" he demanded.

"No, sir, not at all. I'm helping Mr. Ardall and Mrs. Avery for the time being. We thought it would be useful to put two minds to work investigating the matter."

"This is the worst thing that could have happened. With Victor gone, all my plans are up in smoke," he said, lifting his arms to demonstrate smoke floating upward.

"Why is that?" I asked.

"Because without Victor there is no way I can continue to pursue the company. Without Victor everything stops."

"Again, sir, why?"

He glared again. His dark eyes glittered like a raptor's. "It's just over, that's all. And now the stock will plummet and what I've bought will never recoup its value, or if it does it will take years. This situation just simply could not be worse."

"Would the board of directors or Mrs. Avery be willing to work with you on a transition?" I asked. "Don't you own enough stock to move forward with your plans to assume leadership of the company?"

"No, not yet. You can be sure Sally won't give me the time of day. And the board is loyal to Victor. They've been unwilling to sell me stock from the get-go. So no, I'm just fucked."

He was talking to himself, now, heedless of the language he used. "Victor's death is the absolute last thing I needed."

"I'm sorry for your loss," I said, certain that the loss he was mourning was not his brother, but his planned vengeance against that brother.

"Thank you," he said automatically.

"Please convey our sympathy to your wife and children," I said.

"They aren't here," he said. "They were plan-

ning on staying home until this business was finished. It was only supposed to take a couple of
months. I'm on my own here."

Ellis shook his head and lowered his face onto
the palms of his hands. He began to weep.

"Please," he said through his hands.

I told him we wouldn't intrude any further,
thanked him for his willingness to see us at this
difficult time, and Thorne and I walked outside
into the vibrant sunshine and the sour tang of the
trees.

≈11≈

"Don't you adore narcissists?" I asked Thorne as we were driving away. "Victor's death is so utterly inconvenient for Ellis."

"He's a jerk, yes, but genuinely angry."

"I have to agree. But if he didn't profit by the death, does that mean he couldn't have had anything to do with it?"

"We can't rule Ellis out. But Victor would never let Ellis in the house without me there."

"I wonder what really happened between the brothers. Was the conflict there from the time they were little?"

"No idea."

"Did you notice he wasn't wearing a wedding ring? Have you ever met his family?" I asked.

"No. You don't think he's married?"

"There were no toys, no backpacks, no running shoes lying around, so I figured he was in the house by himself. But I wonder why he didn't mention his wife's name. I think most people would say a spouse's name rather than 'they were planning on staying home.' Wouldn't you think? Like 'Martha and the kids'?"

"Maybe."

"In any event, if Ellis isn't the one who caused the explosion, where does that leave us?"

"Hungry," he said.

"You're right, it's lunchtime. I know a place."

א א א

Sitting in a booth at the East-West Café in Daly City, we looked at our menus and ordered. He was having the Blubbery Pan Kakes and I was having the Tie Stake Salade.

Rose, who owns the café, is from the Philippines and she hand-letters the menu each day and runs off copies in her miniscule office at the side of the open kitchen.

The food is fresh and inventive, the restaurant is spotless, and napkins are cloth. The spelling is by ear rather than by dictionary, but Rose knows her mangled vocabulary makes her patrons happy. We treat the menus as entertainment.

"Chip thought Ellis was buying stock from the board members, but Ellis says no. If that's the case, where was he buying it?" I asked, after we'd ordered.

I was sipping hot jasmine tea. Rose brews it from leaves and boiling water and brings it in a ceramic pot to the table. Thorne was drinking iced tea. His forehead glistened a little.

We were in Daly City, a perennial fog zone where the temperature rarely topped sixty-five degrees Fahrenheit. Why was Thorne perspiring?

"Were there enough privately held shares to put Ellis over the fifty percent mark?" I asked. I wanted to know if Ellis could have eventually bought his way to a majority share of the company.

"No," Thorne said. "He could force a seat on the board, yes, but not take over without Victor's shares."

"I don't get it," I said. "If only minor shareholders were selling, he couldn't have built up that much of a holding."

The food arrived, and we ate. I'm always happiest when someone else cooks and does the dishes. Chips and salsa or chateaubriand, if you cook it and clean up afterward I'm in heaven. If, like Rose, you keep adding boiling water to the teapot, I'm transported to a truly wonderful world.

"We have to find Natalie," I said, after swallowing a bite of the salad Rose made from beef, mint, cilantro, shredded cabbage and rice noodles. "Natalie's the missing link here."

"Yes," he said, dipping fruit-filled pancakes into genuine maple syrup.

"How are we going to find her?" I asked. "You're the one who's been living at the Avery's. What do you know about Natalie that would lead us to her if she's not in rehab up in Marin?"

He gave me a look while he bit off a mouthful of bacon.

"Oh duh," I said. "Her mother is how we find her."

He nodded.

"A stakeout. Hooray, I've heard they're tons of fun. Well, we can't use the Porsche. There's no being inconspicuous in that thing with that license plate," I said. "We can use my car. It's new and it won't look out of place in Presidio Terrace."

We finished lunch, split the check, and discovered that we both share the religious conviction that overtipping is one of the secrets to all good things in this world.

As we headed outside, I looked at Thorne and noticed that his forehead was beaded with sweat. Here in Daly City's fogville the sun was struggling and might win out at some point, but it was chilly after the heat of Woodside.

"How are you feeling right now?" I asked him.

"I've been better," he said.

"What is it? Pain?"

"Pain, yes. And fever."

The miracle here is that he was not waving me off and assuring me he was fine, fine, nothing's wrong. This man seemed incapable of macho posturing, or pretense of any kind for that matter.

I put the back of my hand to his forehead. "You need a doctor, big guy. This is what Patrick warned us about. Fever means there's infection and you need antibiotics."

He thought for a moment. "Wait," he said, climbing into the car.

He took out Victor's cell phone and made a call. "Chip?" he said. "I need a doctor who won't report a bullet wound."

He listened for a few seconds, said "Thanks," and put the phone in his pocket.

"Where are we headed?" I asked.

"Chip is setting me up with a doctor friend. He said no blow jobs would be necessary, unless I really wanted to. You head over to keep an eye on Sally."

"I have to take the dogs out anyway," I agreed. I deduced from the blow job remark that Thorne was straight. But of course whether he was straight or gay was none of my business, and our partnership was going to remain platonic because it was one thing to help out a poor schlub in need and another thing entirely to fall for him and make the same mistakes all over again that I'd made too many times already.

Forget it. Not a chance. Never never never. No freaking way. Even though he was literally wounded and needed literal mending. But anyway I really mean it.

≈12≈

I was sitting in my car, a third of the way around the Presidio Terrace circle from the Avery house. It was one-thirty in the afternoon, and I had no idea whether Sally was home or not. In the hour and a half I'd been waiting, no one had entered or left the mansion.

I had brought my book, plus a couple of spares on my phone since I'm a fast reader, and I was reading rather than watching the house. I figured I would notice if the gate opened and a car drove out.

The image of the Fool card kept interrupting my reading. There are many different tarot deck designs; almost every country and culture has a tarot. Some designs are abstract, some are figurative, and some are a combination.

The best-known deck, called the Rider pack,

depicts the Fool as a tunic-clad youth, a bindle stiff striding cheerfully and heedlessly in bright sunshine toward the edge of a cliff. A little dog stands up on its hind legs and barks at him. In my current deck the Fool is a naked infant reaching for low-hanging fruit as a grey wolf watches.

The Fool card can mean someone who is left in isolation, or someone whose brighter and more capable friends or kinfolk must rescue him from disaster when his own wit and resources are not up to the job. It can mean someone who has lost her sanity, or who has abandoned staid thinking for something newer and better. It can refer to what we'd rather not remember about ourselves but would do better not to forget. It can mean original, subtle, sudden impulses or impacts coming from a completely strange quarter. It can describe willfulness driven by evil intentions or folly over which we have no control.

I was trying to fit any of these interpretations into the puzzle of Victor Avery's death. I realized that there was an impetus to what had happened, something that was driving the events but that Thorne and I had not yet unearthed.

The Fool is a trickster; he hides sources and meaning. What did we not yet know about Victor and his family? Who in the family knew what these core facts were?

Meanwhile, what did the Fool mean for me? What was I forgetting about myself that I had better remember? What was I getting myself into that someone smarter than I would have to bail me out of?

The door to the passenger seat opened suddenly. "Hey!" I said, scared, and then I saw the buff work boots and the pants as jolly green Thorne climbed in next to me.

"Hey back," he said.

"All better?" I asked.

"Some better," he answered. "Doctor Pellegrino did all the stuff Patrick wanted us to do that we didn't. He found some yellow shirt in the wound."

"Gak," I said.

"Gak," he agreed. He was silent for a minute. "I liked that shirt," he added.

"Enough to wear it both inside and outside you?" I asked.

He shook his head no.

Neither of us gave the slightest indication that this exchange had been anything but serious. I couldn't believe he was getting my jokes. Well, they weren't jokes; but he got it that I was not being serious and few others ever seemed to regard my humorousness as such.

"No news on this front," I said. "Nobody in or out."

We sat in amicable silence. I offered him a book, which he declined. I offered him his choice of satellite radio stations, which he declined. I let him know that one of the stations was all-Elvis, all the time, and he declined again, although he had the sense to remind me that Elvis is King.

"He sang every song ever written," I said.

"Not 'MacArthur Park.'"

"I beg to differ," I replied. "There's an out-of-print three-CD set on which he is clearly heard to warble that someone has left the cake out in the rain, and he will never find the recipe again."

"Oh no-o-o-o-oh," we sang in unison. We sounded like coyotes.

"I think that proves beyond any doubt that he was under the influence of brain-destroying, albeit prescription, pharmaceuticals," I said.

"Right now I am," Thorne said, "and I just sang 'MacArthur Park'."

"Well, albeit and all, Elvis was otherwise a paragon of good taste and good sense. The Jungle Room and the fried banana sandwiches indicate this in no uncertain terms. I think we can forgive one small lapse. Albeit."

He reached for the seat controls and reclined almost as far as the seat would go, pushing the seat backward at the same time so his knees weren't jammed up against the glove compartment.

Given his Kong-like size, the reclined seat made good sense. Someone looking out from the Avery mansion would not see his head stretching up to the interior roof of the car.

"You're going to fall asleep from the prescription pharmaceuticals," I said.

"Am not," he said.

"Are too."

"Am not."

And he didn't, because the Avery's driveway gate slid open and the silver Jaguar drove out with Sally behind the wheel.

We pulled out after her, heading right on Arguello to California and turning left toward downtown. I kept two or three cars in between us, but she didn't seem interested in her mirrors, and she drove straight ahead, across Van Ness Avenue and up Nob Hill.

On Nob Hill, just before California Street dropped downhill to the Financial District, she turned into the forecourt of the Mark Hopkins Hotel and gave the Jaguar to the valet. She handed him something from her purse, and he backed the Jag into a slot next to a white Rolls Royce.

I stopped at the corner and let Thorne out. We decided I was dressed for the Mark and he wasn't, so he climbed into the driver's seat and drove around the block while I headed inside. He would continue driving around the block until I called him or came out; you'd need a rain slicker in the Sahara before you'd ever find street parking on Nob Hill.

"Good afternoon," said the doorman, opening the door into the lobby.

"Good afternoon," I replied, striding in to the surprisingly small lobby.

The Mark's august reputation is well earned. Sconces with pleated raw silk shades cast glowing golden light over the carpets and furniture. The lobby is peach walls and cognac leather and mahogany tables, with deep sofas in velvet and striped silk. There are tall vases of flowers next to plush armchairs that look like you could sink down to sea level if you dropped onto one.

I went to the front desk.

"Welcome to the Mark Hopkins," said a handsome young man in a beautiful suit. The name plate on his jacket read Christopher.

"Hello. My name is Lorraine Higgins and I'm supposed to meet Mrs. Avery. Mrs. Victor Avery? Should I use the house phone to call her?"

"I'll ring her room for you," he offered.

"Thank you."

"My pleasure," he said. I didn't think he would find it pleasurable, but it had to be done.

He typed on his computer, reached for the phone, and I watched him press 71820. Through the phone I heard a deep male voice answer hello.

"Ms. Lorraine Higgins is here to see Mrs. Avery," Christopher said. "Shall I send her up?"

I felt sorry for what was about to happen to Christopher. He was a perfectly nice person doing his job with exquisite courtesy.

He held the phone away from his ear when the male voice boomed "No! No calls and no visitors!"

"I beg your pardon, sir. There must be a misunderstanding," he said, and hung up.

"Oh dear," I said. "I'm sure it's my mistake.

I'll call her cell phone. Maybe I've got the day mixed up. Thank you so much for your help." I turned and headed out the door, swept open by the obliging doorman.

"Oh, I forgot something," I said, smiling foolishly, reversing and walking to a house phone by the elevators. I dialed 71820. There was no answer for four rings, and then I heard the angry bass voice.

"I said no calls!" he shouted and slammed down the phone, but before he hung up I heard two loud female voices in the background. One sounded like Sally's. The other was a hoarse shriek.

The doorman and I exchanged good afternoons again, and I walked to the corner to wait for Thorne.

"She's in room eighteen-twenty," I said when he picked me up. "There's a man answering the phone who refused the call and said no visitors. He has a deep voice and a surly manner."

"Surly?"

"Definitely surly. Do you have any idea who it might be?"

"None."

"I think we have to ask Sally about that. It's my guess Natalie's staying there with some kind of guard. I heard another woman with a voice that was kind of croaky yelling at Sally."

He parked the car next to a fire hydrant and we watched the hotel entrance. Across California

Street from the Mark Hopkins the many colorful flags lining the front of the Fairmont Hotel were flapping in the early afternoon breeze.

The sun was shining on this, the eastern side of town, but the four o'clock wind would kick in later. San Francisco is surrounded on three sides by water: the Pacific Ocean to the west, the Golden Gate to the north, and San Francisco Bay to the east.

Beyond San Francisco Bay, Oakland and Berkeley and the rest of the East Bay heat up by day and push the fog out to sea. The land mass cools off in the afternoon and sucks the marine layer—aka the marrow-chilling fog—across the City at speeds that can gust up to twenty to thirty miles per hour.

Particularly active during the hottest months, this geographic fluke creates San Francisco's air conditioning system, with the moisture scrubbing the smog out of our air as it congeals the visiting Nebraskans in their Bermuda shorts and tank tops and flip flops, who expect August to be hot.

Through chattering teeth these pitiful goose-pimpled specimens look so surprised and forlorn that we locals point the way to the nearest Eddie Bauer and its year-round selection of down jackets. I've been known to escort them there personally if it looks like frostbite is setting in.

א א א

The four o'clock wind was buffeting the car and the fog was streaming eastward overhead by the time Sally emerged from the hotel. Thorne touched my arm and I woke up. Oops. It turns out stakeouts are a lot like taking Ambien. In my defense, I hadn't slept in thirty-six hours.

I stretched and yawned and started the car, following Sally to Presidio Terrace. When we saw her driving into her gate Thorne got out by the Porsche and drove in after her. He was going to stay at the mansion that night. I had programmed his cell number into my phone.

I was heading home to take care of the dogs and get some more sleep. I planned to return in the morning to talk to Sally. We hadn't made the decision yet whether to go to the Mark and knock on the door of room 1820 tonight or tomorrow, after we talked to Sally. We'd wait to see if she went out again tonight. If she did, Thorne would call me and we'd meet up en route.

So that was the idea until I pulled into the garage and picked up the mail from the basket hanging below the mail slot in the garage door. A white envelope caught my eye; my name had been hand-lettered on the envelope but there was no address. I lifted the flap and took out a note, printed in turquoise ink: STAY OUT OF THE AVERY BUSINESS OR YOU WILL BE SORRY.

≈*13*≈

The hair at the back of my head tingled, but the turquoise ink and the passed-to-me-during-study-hall wording of the note were less chilling once I got upstairs and the dogs and cats hurried to greet me. It reminded me of how Thorne said Ellis had threatened Victor.

"Yes, I am the one with the food and the key to the great outdoors," I assured the pets, dropping the note on the kitchen counter. I let the dogs out into their side-yard run and put some crunchies in the cat food dish.

Reaching for the phone to call Thorne with the news of the note, I saw the message light blinking on the answering machine. Pushing play, I first heard a message from Patrick asking about our patient. I'd have to call him back. Then I heard my mother's voice: "Alexandra, just a reminder dear, I'll be arriving at six-thirty this evening and staying over after the symphony. Would you like to join us for a late supper?"

Oh, crap. I'd forgotten my mother was scheduled to come up this evening from Pebble Beach and spend the night. She likes golf more than anything else on earth, but when she feels the urge for capital-C Culture she snares an invitation to the symphony or the opera from one of her socialite pals who live in the City or Hillsborough. She likes to stay with me on these occasions; hence the new guest room two stories down from where I sleep.

Sharing a bathroom with my mother is a daunting prospect. She primps at length. She prefers not to re-use hand towels. Until now, when she stayed for more than a day I've had to run the washing machine more often than the parents of a newborn.

I threw my red leather jacket onto a chair, ran down the stairs and stripped and remade the guest room bed, pushed the furniture back where it belonged, and changed the bathroom towels. I added five hand towels to the rack and set down a rattan basket for the damp discards.

I opened a little box of almond-scented soaps formed into shell-shapes and arranged them in a porcelain dish on the sink. I filled a lidded carafe with filtered water and positioned it on the nightstand next to a crystal old-fashioned glass. I was panting from running up and down the stairs to the kitchen and the laundry, but when the doorbell rang everything was ready.

"Hello, my dear," said Louisa Duncan Livingston Monaghan Bard of Darien, Connecticut, grasping my shoulders in a firm grip and aiming an air-kiss at the vicinity of my right cheekbone. No hugging allowed.

My mother is petite, exquisitely groomed, faultlessly attired, expensively educated, and entirely uninterested in anyone but herself.

"Hello, Mother. How was your drive?"

"All those people in their SUVs should be summarily executed and buried in deep, unmarked communal graves," she said, handing me her overnight suitcase and garment bag. The suitcase was a medium-sized red Samsonite, circa 1975, without wheels. Wheels are apparently not the done thing in Pebble Beach.

Like many old-school WASPs, Mater buys only the best, at full retail price, does nothing to maintain what she buys, uses things until they disintegrate decades after she purchased them, and then complains that there is no craftsmanship any more.

I led Mater down the ground-floor hall to the door of the new guest room.

"It's finished?" she asked, walking in. "Ah, I see, it's finished," she answered herself, looking around and walking into the bathroom.

"It's nice, dear," she said, smiling her compliment smile, her coral lipstick painted precisely onto the lips of her small mouth.

"Now don't do a thing for me," she said, meaning the opposite. "I'm going to change clothes and DeDe is picking me up at seven."

I put her overnight case on the luggage stand and her garment bag in the closet. "Would you like a little something?" I asked, using her euphemism for a highball.

"Is there any scotch? Just a taste, very light, on the rocks with lots of water." Saying this like it was a sudden whim, like she hadn't been slugging down the same exact drink, one after the other all evening long, for the last fifty years.

"Dewars," I said. "Especially for you." I can't explain the plebeian choice. I think perhaps there is some frugal Yankee thing in action there. Maybe it's because she adds ice and water and doesn't want to waste the expensive stuff by doing that. Who knows? I am not about to ask.

I let the dogs in and went upstairs to make her a drink. By the time I came downstairs with it she had unpacked and changed into a midnight blue silk georgette dress with bugle beads glistening on the collar and sleeves. Sitting on the teak chair, she was pulling on *peau de soie* evening sandals. She operates at full-speed-ahead, does Ms. Louisa, and her stamina would compare favorably with sled dogs running the Iditarod.

She took the drink and swallowed some, and put the glass down on the nightstand on the coaster I pulled out of the drawer.

"Did I hear you let the dogs in? Could you keep them upstairs while I'm here? They do shed so."

I had changed the duvet on the bed, or she would have seen ample evidence to support her claim.

"I've got them shut in the kitchen," I said.

"The cats as well? I hate being allergic, but I won't submit to those horrible shots."

"They're up in my room, and I'll keep them upstairs while you're here."

She had her compact out and was adjusting her makeup. "Oh, I forgot my wrap. Would you be a dear?" She handed me her car keys. "I parked in the driveway."

In San Francisco, it is uniformly known and accepted that blocking someone's driveway justifies the aggrieved party in running the nuclear launch codes.

More than three quarters of the block on my side of 48th Avenue is parkside, with no houses or garages. A hundred-yard stretch of gray curb, entirely empty of automobiles, sits adjacent to my driveway. At least she left me her car keys this time.

I moved her Cadillac and then opened the rear door to retrieve her sable jacket in its zippered bag, on its padded hanger. I brought it in as she was tucking her compact and lipstick into an elaborately embroidered evening clutch.

The room smelled of hairspray. Ice was all

that remained in the highball glass.

"What time will the symphony be over?" I asked.

"End, dear. You know I hate it when people put a preposition at the end of a sentence. It usually ends around ten. What do you think about joining us for a late supper? I know Charlotte and Ann would love to see you. DeDe as well." She reached into her overnight bag and pulled out a pair of three-button navy kid gloves.

"I'd love to see them too," I said, realizing that for once my mother's clenched-jaw seven-sisters crowd might prove useful.

"And you'll wear a nice dress?" she reminded me, as if without her coaching I would deck myself out like Emmett Kelly, or maybe like Cher, with tattooed ass cheeks hanging out and a feather headdress.

We agreed I would meet her at Absinthe at ten-fifteen, and the doorbell rang. DeDe's driver, Hillyard, was waiting there. We said hello, and I held my mother's jacket for her as she slipped into the cloudlike softness of the fur. The color of the sable matched her carefully dyed and coiffed hair.

Mater put her hand on top of Hillyard's as she stepped down and into the rear seat of a pewter-colored Bentley. DeDe and I waved at each other as Hillyard closed the door behind my mother, who tucked her skirt carefully under herself as she settled onto the stitched pearl gray leather with dark gray piping.

Off they went down Anza Street, two wealthy patrons of the arts, off to patronize.

Now, are there any lingering questions about the psychotherapy bills?

I thought not.

≈14≈

I called Thorne and told him about the note. He said Sally hadn't gone out again.

"Should I come over there?" He was asking whether I was worried about the note.

"My mother is staying here tonight. Nobody in his right mind would take Mater on."

"You call her Mater?"

"Not to her face."

"Ah. Of course. So what's your plan?"

"Actually, she's gone out with some friends who probably know all about the Averys. She asked me to join them after the symphony. I'm going to see what they can tell me about the family."

"Call me."

I told him I would, and I went up to my room and slept for an hour. When the alarm buzzed I took a shower and changed into a dress and heels. I tinkered with my makeup and jewelry and hair until I thought I would pass muster with the wolf pack Mater runs with.

At ten o'clock I was sitting at the table reserved for the symphony gals, and fifteen minutes later in they walked, chirping like house wrens, handing their furs to the woman at the coat check. Each of mother's friends held out both manicured, bejeweled hands to clasp mine as they approached the table. The aroma of Joy and Shalimar and Chanel No. 5 preceded them. None of those Britney or Jennifer fragrances for this old-school quartet.

"Don't you look lovely," Ann said. "Doesn't she look lovely, Louisa." It was not a question. We sat down and began cooing the required civilities.

"Her blonde hair looks so pretty when she wears black," Charlotte said to my mother, as if my mother deserved the praise.

"And I love the necklace," DeDe said. "The citrines and the pearls keep the black from being too drab. I think it's so difficult not to look drab in black."

"Thank you, DeDe," I said. "Is that Ungaro you're wearing? His florals are so feminine, and they suit you so perfectly."

Whatever they serve at you, it's essential to hit it back across the net. Otherwise you're "not contributing to the conversation."

The waiter arrived and we ordered drinks: more scotch for mother, Dubonnet on the rocks for Ann, cognac for DeDe and white wine for Charlotte. I already had a sparkling water with lime.

"Now tell us what you've been up to," Charlotte commanded. The good thing about the rules these ladies live by is that I was raised abiding by them. I knew my job was to provide the second round of entertainment for the evening.

"It's a long story, but I've been trying to find out what happened to Victor Avery."

"*So* shocking!" Ann said. "Victor was such a *love*."

"That family has certainly had some difficulties," DeDe added, with a nod to Ann. The drinks arrived and there was silence while the waiter set them down. It is not the done thing to let the servants hear one gossiping.

"Chin chin!" DeDe toasted, and we clinked glasses and sipped.

"I'm hoping you can tell me what you know about the Averys," I said. "What happened between the brothers?"

They exchanged looks, and by some unspoken balloting process Charlotte was elected. Before she could begin, however, the waiter reappeared. We ordered and he went away.

Charlotte gathered her thoughts and sat back, swirling the wine in her wineglass slowly.

"Veronica and Charles had two boys, Victor

first and then a few years later Ellis."

The other women nodded their agreement.

"From the first, Charles groomed Victor as his heir. After all, he was the first-born, a son, and there was no way of knowing another boy would come along."

DeDe seemed to think an explanation was required. "I know things have changed since the women's movement, but it was forty years ago and this was how things were done then." I managed not to appear shocked by this revelation.

"When Ellis arrived, he was a little less of a natural star than Victor," Charlotte continued. "Charles really didn't pay very much attention to him. Ellis became Veronica's and Victor belonged to Charles. Veronica overprotected Ellis, I would say. He was smaller than Victor at first because he was younger, and I don't think he ever caught up in size."

"He didn't," Mater said. "He's about five-nine. Victor was at least six feet."

"Yes, he was tall. Tall, dark, and handsome," DeDe said. "He was quite a catch, in his day." She looked wistful.

"Why did Ellis disappear?" I asked.

"Oh, he was a terrible disappointment," Ann chimed in. "Veronica told me Charles was always after Ellis about his grades. And they caught him in the liquor cabinet when he was fourteen, refilling the vodka bottles with water! He'd been drinking vodka, for heaven's sake! At *fourteen*!"

It was now confirmed that these women had never kept up with Oprah. Well, of course not. Oprah had not gone to Vassar.

"He was always in some trouble or other," Charlotte said. "Girls and booze and nasty pranks at school. He was nice-looking and he had money, and girls who liked boys who were supposed to be dangerous used to be attracted to him. He went to Saint Ignatius, and then to St, Paul's, and then Lawrenceville, and then—where was it—the Hill School?"

"That's right. They finally managed to get Ellis into Princeton," Charlotte said, "but only because Charles donated a science lab or an auditorium or something. The Averys all went to Princeton, and Victor did very well there, but Ellis was asked to leave during his freshman year."

"Why?" I asked.

My mother grabbed the baton and ran with it. "He got very drunk one night and drove onto the dean's lawn at four o'clock in the morning. He was completely squiffed, honking his horn until the dean called the police.

"It turns out he'd been caught the previous afternoon cheating on a midterm and was suspended pending a disciplinary hearing," Mater continued. "Ellis was shouting that everybody cheated at Princeton, and he was the only one to get caught. He was sent home later that same morning. He was only eighteen. Or was he nineteen? Didn't he repeat a grade because of all the switching around from school to school?" The consensus among the ladies seemed to be yes on that one.

"Then what?" I asked.

"Charles and Veronica sent him to Europe," said Charlotte. "He was there for three or four years, I think."

Our food arrived and we began to eat. One of the rules of my mother's crowd is that dinner table conversation continues uninterrupted by dinner, so between small, manageable bites eaten while my elbows remained off the table I asked, "Why Europe?"

"It's what one did in those days," Charlotte answered. "One sent away the errant offspring with enough money to live decently and with the understanding that he or she was not to return unless summoned. Sometimes that approach actually worked. But it didn't with Ellis."

Using her knife and fork, she took a small, manageable bite of her salad.

Ann said, "We heard nothing about him for years. We had to tiptoe around the subject with Veronica and Charles. 'How is Ellis?' we'd ask, and they'd answer 'Fine,' and we had to drop the subject after that. We asked about Victor instead, and Charles would go on and on about how Victor was learning the business, and what a natural he was, and how proud he was of him."

"Then Ellis came home uninvited," DeDe said. "There were rumors that he'd gotten into some scrape in Italy and the *carabinieri* were going to arrest him."

"Wasn't Victor married by then?" Ann asked.

"Yes," Charlotte said, "but he and Sally were living in New York somewhere. Weren't they up near Albany?"

"That's right. Avery Chemical had a big plant up there, on the Hudson near Troy, and he was managing it. Water-something. Watervliet? Some Dutch name. I don't think the brothers saw each other when Ellis came home."

They all shook their heads no.

"He wasn't home long enough," DeDe said.

"Anyway, Ellis came back and Veronica prevailed on Charles to give him another chance, but that didn't last," Mother said. "By then Ellis had been living on his own for years, and he was over twenty-one, so he was staying out late and drinking and doing God knows what else. One night he brought a girl home and when she came down to the breakfast table with him, that was it for Veronica."

"Charles cut him off without a penny," DeDe said.

Charlotte said, "Nobody seems to care about sex anymore, but in our day parents thought those sorts of shenanigans were inexcusable. Ellis couldn't have done anything more certain to offend his parents."

"Veronica was heartbroken," Ann said. "She realized it was impossible to have Ellis at home, but she wanted Charles to continue his allowance.

Charles said Ellis hadn't any sense, and maybe having to earn a living would force him to develop some. Ellis dropped out of sight and nobody heard from him again until he showed up this past January."

"He's rented the glass house in Woodside, hasn't he?" asked DeDe.

"Yes," Charlotte said. "From the Laughtons. When he signed the lease he told them his family would be joining him, but I haven't heard that anyone has seen a family there."

"Where did he get the money to rent the house, do you know?" I asked.

"Nobody knows," DeDe whispered, and the ladies all shook their heads at this. In their world, one is supposed to know where everybody else's money comes from.

"Do you know who's been selling him stock?"

"No," Charlotte answered. "Rumor has it that he's been buying, but not from anyone we know. On the open market, is my guess."

DeDe chimed in. "Nobody thinks Ellis should be given control of that company. He'd run it straight into the ground."

"He's trying to settle an old score with Victor," Ann said.

"Well, I guess he's got free rein, now," Mater said. "With Victor gone, Ellis will prevail."

"That's not what he said today," I said.

"*What*! You saw Ellis Avery?"

They leaned forward, salad forks forgotten on

their plates, with an avidity that would have been unseemly had they not been gleaming with such tasteful diamonds.

"Ellis said the deal was off, now that Victor was dead," I told them. "He said there was no way he could proceed with the takeover now."

"This is just a rumor, but I heard something about Bix Bonebreak making a move on Victor," Charlotte said. She twiddled her salad fork on her empty plate. I looked at her but she wouldn't look up. There was a sudden chill of tension. DeDe's face glowed a bright pink. My mother glared at Charlotte.

The busboy took our salad plates away and the waiter put three different desserts on the table, with five dessert forks. The ladies picked up the forks and their bites became even daintier, but the chocolate *pot de crème*, blueberry tart and raspberry flan disappeared steadily.

"Sally won't sell her shares?" DeDe asked me.

"Ellis said no, she wouldn't."

Watching them eat the desserts was like watching air-traffic-controlled airplanes lining up to land. Their forks glided in turn from plate to mouth at precisely managed intervals, with no hint of a potential collision.

"I don't know," Charlotte said. "I wouldn't be so sure of what Sally will do." Without looking at each other, in unison, they arched their eyebrows. They were the Olympic precision eyebrow team.

"Why do you say that?" I asked them.

"Well, Sally, after all," my mother said, and they all nodded as if the meaning of this non-pronouncement couldn't have been clearer.

"You'll have to help me," I said. "Sally what?"

"You must give her credit, Louisa," Charlotte said. "She's done everything she possibly could to make Victor happy and not embarrass him. She made it her business to not push."

Charlotte turned to me. "She taught herself how to speak, how to decorate her home, where to send Natalie to school. She attended events to which Victor was invited but she didn't try to shove her way in where she wasn't wanted. Of course they came to the events one doesn't miss—the opening of the opera and the symphony every September, that sort of thing. It was mostly her clothes that stood in her way."

DeDe agreed. "She wore Passion perfume, for goodness' sake! I tried to give her a little hint about it but she said Victor liked it. But you're right, it was the clothes more than anything."

"What about them?" I asked.

"It was very clear what the attraction was for Victor," my mother said, barely avoiding sniffing in disgust. "Sally knew Victor found her sexy. Well, good Lord, the men fell all over themselves around her, and all these years later she's still dressing like a sexpot. Everything tight and cling-ing, those vivid colors that draw your attention. It's too too too. Don't you remember that slit-down-to-here gown she wore to the Black-and-

White Ball? It was *Gucci* for heaven's sake! It was in both the papers."

As far as my mother is concerned, only climbers and criminals wind up with their names in the papers. Thank God there's only one major San Francisco daily remaining; it cuts in half the risk of her name appearing in anything but an obituary.

"She doesn't have to work very hard at being sexy," I said. "She's gorgeous."

"If you like having it thrown in your face," Mother said. I refrained from remarking that it was difficult to find any men who didn't like it that way and any women who liked seeing another woman throwing it faceward.

I remembered Sally Stanford, the infamous bordello keeper in pre-World War II San Francisco, who went on to become mayor of Sausalito and after that ran a waterfront restaurant there. Sally was not the sort of name a proper San Franciscan gave to a daughter.

"What do you know about Natalie?" I asked. Natalie, as names go, would pass.

"Natalie was darling," Ann said. "She had beautiful big brown eyes and that shiny black hair. She always looked like a china doll. Victor adored her."

"But she ran away last year, and these past few months she's been having problems," I said. "What happened?"

"No one knows," DeDe said, carefully skewering a raspberry on the tines of her dessert fork. "We're guessing she's boy crazy, but nobody knows who the boy is."

"How old was she when Victor and Sally married?"

"Three or four? Maybe five?" Charlotte looked at the others for agreement and they nodded.

"Victor adopted her," she continued. "I assumed she was fatherless. I've never heard otherwise, and there've been no visits from a birth father. Her parents come here to visit, don't they? The Averys haven't ever gone to New Jersey, have they? To visit Sally's parents?"

They shook their heads no at Charlotte.

"Did Victor know Sally while he was at Princeton?" I asked.

"It's very unlikely," Charlotte said. "I think she grew up in New Jersey somewhere, but she's at least five years younger than Victor. And I don't think she grew up near the college."

"She says she grew up in Trenton."

"Oh. Well, that's not far geographically, but it might as well be light years away when you're at Princeton."

"What about Ellis? Could he have known her?"

"I suppose anything is possible," Charlotte answered. "They're closer in age. But she would have been a townie. The Princetonians and the townies don't mix very much. And anyway Ellis wasn't there that long. Only the first few months of his freshman year."

All that remained of the three desserts was a smear of raspberry sauce and a few chocolate cookie crumbs.

"Shall we have some espresso?" Ann asked.

"If you like," my mother said.

The women looked at each other and, by some mystical communion, agreed to forego coffee. I know that's what happened, but even using tarot cards I couldn't begin to explain how it worked.

"Whose turn is it?" DeDe asked.

"Let's make it my turn," Mother said. "I'd like to treat Alexandra. She's always so good about letting me stay with her. And she's made such a pleasant guest room out of her garage out there at the ocean. Now I don't have to go up and down all those steps."

In the *patois* of her set, she was saying I had relegated her to a dank, gasoline-smelling dungeon and refused to let her occupy the, by comparison, more salubrious upper floors of my inconvenient house.

"You know you're welcome to stay with any of us at any time, Louisa," DeDe said, quick to the rescue.

Ann and Charlotte both agreed. Since they all lived in houses with a minimum of fifteen rooms, in Sea Cliff and Hillsborough and Presidio Heights, it's safe to say there would be space for Mater, should she choose to avail herself of it.

"Oh, aren't you sweet, but I couldn't think of it," Mother said. "This way I get to have a nice visit with Alexandra, and I'm so proud of what she's done with her house."

She made it sound like I had molded a slightly less lumpy ashtray than is typical during arts and crafts period in kindergarten.

א א א

"Who is Bix Bonebreak?" I asked.

"Why are you involved with this Victor Avery business?" Mater asked in non-response as we drove homeward on Fulton Street through the Western Addition. She looked straight ahead out the windshield, on the alert for hazards and keeping me informed about them as I drove. Red lights counted as hazards.

"A friend of mine worked for Victor. He thinks the death was suspicious, and I'm helping him talk to people."

"Why?" she pressed, pulling the sable around her with gloved hands as she waited for the heater to warm up the car.

"Because it feels like the right thing to do," I said, measuring my words and suppressing an urge to apologize for myself. "I don't believe Mr. Avery's death was an accident."

"You're not being foolish again, are you?" This was a reference to my perceived failures in the romance department.

"Perhaps, but not in the way you mean," I said.

"I hope not," she said. "I do worry about you."

"Who is Bix Bonebreak?" I asked again, remembering DeDe's blush, "and what does he have to do with DeDe?"

I had to outwait her. We drove steadily through the timed lights as we approached the northern edge of Golden Gate Park.

Resigned and resentful, she said, "Bix Bonebreak is the insufferable boor DeDe had a little fling with when she was just out of college."

"Why is he still a sore topic?"

More silence. "It took time for DeDe to realize the affair couldn't really go anywhere."

The dawn of understanding broke. Mater had scotched the relationship somehow.

"Is she still in touch with him?" I asked.

"DeDe was only widowed this past year," Mother insisted.

"All right, but that's not what I asked you. In any case, why would this man Bix be involved in Victor Avery's situation?"

"Bix owns a scrap metal company. In his own way, he's become quite successful," she said.

She meant he was very rich, and she begrudged him his wealth after predicting to DeDe that he had no future.

"If he's a potential rival of Mr. Avery's, I'd like to talk to him," I said.

"Why on earth would you need to do that? He's so unpleasant!" *Unpleasant* is the roughest pejorative Mater ever applies to anyone.

"I don't know enough about what was going on with the Avery business yet," I said. "I have to keep asking questions of anyone who might know something until I can figure out what happened." It sounded unconvincing, even to me.

Mater looked over at me. "I know there's no stopping you once you get a fixed idea in your head. But Bix Bonebreak is not someone you would ever want to annoy. He is a very unsavory person. He has hoodlums who do things for him. If you plan to see him I want you to call me afterward."

I have learned to count my blessings and interpret this sort of declaration as the way she expresses her motherly affection—or anyway what affection she is capable of offering. I agreed to call her after seeing Bix Bonebreak.

Mater's other expression of love is to loan her children money to buy houses and cars, to be repaid at a modest rate of interest. We siblings refer to this process, never to her face, as borrowing from the Bank of Louisa the Loaded. Sometimes Bard Bucks. Sometimes Mater Moolah. You get the idea. We're a little ashamed that we do it, but we do it anyway.

We've compared notes, and not even Brett, the oldest and her favorite, has ever heard her say she loves him. But after many sessions with my helpful shrink, Peter Perriman, Ph.D., I've concluded that love is love, even when it shows up in the guise of a low monthly payment.

א א א

At home I let the dogs out. The cats know from long bitter experience to hide under a sofa or duck behind a cabinet when Mater comes to call.

Wearing a pearl grey cashmere robe over her charcoal silk charmeuse pajamas, she came upstairs to fix herself a nightcap. I heard her high-heeled slippers clicking up the stairs, and before she saw it I slid the threatening turquoise note off the kitchen counter and into my sleeve.

"Thank you for joining us tonight, and thank you for the hospitality," my mother said, sipping from her Waterford tumbler.

"It was good of you to invite me, and sweet of you to treat me to such a delicious dinner, and I'm always happy to see you and your friends." I smiled.

She went downstairs with her scotch and I called Thorne to tell him what I'd gleaned from Mater's cronies. I had an idea—an intuition—that I was confident would pan out. That it did, that I was proved correct, brought me little happiness. It brought nobody happiness, as it turned out. The Fool Card portends adventure, or misadventure, but rarely happiness.

≈15≈

When I woke up the next morning Mater had left. She was an early riser, and one thing in her favor is that she doesn't require me to get up with her at five-thirty. She probably had a golf game at her club to get home to. Or rather, proper preposition-position-wise, to which she needed home to get.

Before I went to bed I had filled the coffee-maker and set out a travel mug for her. It was her habit to stop by the French bakery on Fillmore and pick up a fresh croissant to eat on the drive to Pebble Beach. She had remade the bed and put the used towels on top of the washing machine. In two days I would receive a handwritten thank-you note.

There are worse houseguests than Mater, and if you ever live in San Francisco you will experience ongoing proof of that fact, generally starting when school lets out in June and ending when school starts up again in September.

I called Thorne and asked for the latest.

"Sally is here," he said, "and Natalie isn't."

"I'm on the way over. I need to talk to Sally again. You and I can plan what to do next until she's ready to see us."

The sun was winning the battle with the fog this morning, but the air was still cool even in the bright sunshine. I parked my car in the mansion's lower driveway and climbed the steps to the garden.

Thorne materialized above me, his shadow blocking out the sun. I jumped and made an *eek* sound, and then his big hand was on my arm steadying me. He let go when I reached the top of the steps. He looked me in the eye to be sure I was okay, and I nodded.

On the bricked patio were wet rugs and furniture set out to dry. A tall, metal-legged frame shielded the elegant wood and fabrics under a blue canvas tarpaulin.

We walked to the glass-paned door together. I was wearing a long black knit skirt, black leather walking boots, a black top and a light blue mohair jacket; he was in a clean yellow oxford-cloth shirt and black jeans. He was wearing black and white leather athletic shoes today. Given the flying Michael Jordan outline, I deduced they were basketball shoes.

"You have another yellow shirt," I said.

"I do," he answered as we entered the back hall. There was a vacuum cleaner's drone from the direction of the dining room.

"I told Sally you were on your way," he went on, "and she didn't look happy, but she didn't say no."

We went downstairs to the garage and beyond the parked cars into Thorne's living space. We passed the Porsche and Jaguar in the garage, and Thorne nodded at an apple green VW Cabrio, saying it was Natalie's.

The security equipment and monitors sat on a shelf along the rear wall. A bookcase stacked with labeled security footage stood to the right of the equipment.

The room Thorne lived in was below ground. There were glass block windows along the upper edge of one wall, letting in outdoor light. The space was large—maybe thirty by forty feet or so—and there was a bathroom at the far end.

The ceiling was only eight feet high and he had to duck under the door lintel, but the room itself felt spacious. The walls were a pale butter color, the woodwork a glossy white. A wide set of closet doors spread across one wall. I figured the closet held a Murphy bed.

There was a low chenille-covered sofa, a butcher-block table and chairs, a short countertop with a sink, and above that were glass-front cabinets. A microwave and mini-fridge completed a basic kitchen. It was a short step up from Spartan, but it was well laid out and very clean in an unequivocal way.

"Would you like tea?" Thorne asked.

"Yes, please."

He made tea from teabags and I sipped it, fussing over him a little, asking about the bandage and painkillers and how much sleep he'd gotten and the rate of his recovery.

"I'm fine," he said.

"Do you think Sally will talk to me? It won't be as pleasant this time. And I'm not wearing the red jacket."

He shrugged. We drank our tea and put the mugs in the sink.

We walked upstairs. I could hear a washing machine whirling through its spin cycle. The kitchen windows had been stripped of their drapes. In the dining room a fifty-ish woman in a red velour track suit was vacuuming the rug. Light flooded into the empty room through the wide bay window, shed of its curtains.

When she saw us she turned off the machine and smiled broadly. Thorne introduced me to Lupita in fluent Spanish. I said *mucho gusto*. I asked her in atrocious Spanish whether she had been in the house the night Mr. Avery died, and she said, "No, sorry, I no here tha nigh."

She turned to Thorne and told him in Spanish how terrible *Señor* Victor's accident was, and in equally fluent Spanish he agreed. She said the house would take days and days and much work to clean up. She sympathized with the poor *señora* and the *muchacha*, and Thorne nodded his head. She said she was glad to see him come home again, and he said he was glad to see her as well, and then she was finished. We said adios and headed out to the hall. The vacuum started up again.

The sun-washed living room was cleared down to the hardwood floor. Yellow tape remained strung across the library doorway.

Walking upstairs I asked Thorne about the Spanish. He stopped at the top step with his hand on the banister.

"My mother was from Guadalajara," he said. "I grew up there until I came to the U.S. to go to prep school."

"Your last name isn't Spanish, though."

"No. My dad was a banker from Boston. My full name is Thorne Cadogan Ardall the fourth Rafols. The bank had offices in Guadalajara and my dad met my mother because the bank did business with her father's company. In Mexico, custom dictates that you socialize with business acquaintances."

"Your father is tall?"

"And my mother. She was six feet, he was six four. I have dozens of second and third cousins, all over six feet. I don't see them anymore, but at family get-togethers the household staff used to look like Munchkins."

Jeez. The household staff. What conclusions was I supposed to draw about this fellow? So far, every time I made an assumption, he'd say something that forced me to make a one-eighty and start over again.

He turned and we walked to Sally's sitting room. The door was shut and I knocked.

She opened the door to us, but stood in it, blocking our entry. Today she was wearing black, a pin-tucked knit suit with a mandarin-collar jacket and a pencil skirt hemmed below her knees. She was wearing dark hose, black low-heeled pumps, and her only jewelry besides the rings were pearl stud earrings. Her hair was pulled up into a thick black grosgrain ribbon.

Nothing she had done to herself could minimize her looks. Her clear unlined skin was flawless, and the severe tailoring of the suit was countered by the way the knit fitted her curves. She had used concealer to mask the shadows under her eyes, but any other makeup was minimal.

"I'm afraid today is not a good day," she said, her blue-green eyes hard and unfriendly.

"I apologize for intruding on your privacy," I said. "There's something I have to ask you about Natalie."

"I told you Natalie is not here," she said.

"I think it would be best if you'd sit down, Mrs. Avery," I said. "I'm afraid my questions may prove to be upsetting to you."

"I don't see why I should answer any questions. This is none of your business." She paused and looked at me more closely. "You're that snooty Louisa Bard's daughter, aren't you? My God, how do you *stand* it?"

I felt my cheeks heating up, whether with rage or chagrin I couldn't be sure. Seeing her insult pay off, she tilted her head up so she could look down her nose at me and said, "I'd be grateful if you would leave my house, please." She stepped back and began to shut the door. I was betting she'd learned how to do that from my mother.

"Natalie is Ellis's daughter, isn't she?" I asked.

Sally froze. She stared at the carpet under her feet as if it were utterly fascinating, then looked up to examine me as if I were a bedbug she'd found in her mattress. Should she pound me with her shoe and hope I was the only one, or call someone to come fumigate?

"You met Ellis eighteen years ago at your father's restaurant," I said. "He was with friends. You went out with him that night, and at some point he got very drunk. I'm guessing you might have gotten drunk as well, but maybe it was intoxicating enough to be out with a boy from Princeton. And the next day Ellis disappeared and you were knocked up."

She was going to slam the door in my face, but Thorne had his arm around me and the other one on the door to stop her.

"If Ellis told you that, he's lying," she snarled. Even snarling she looked better than most women look on their wedding day.

"Ellis didn't say anything about it," I said. "But that doesn't mean it's a lie. Ellis looks like Victor. Natalie looks like them both. The question is, does Natalie know who her birth father was? Does Ellis know? Did Victor know?"

"Nobody knows anything of the sort. Now you will leave my home, both of you, or I will call the police."

"I don't think so, Mrs. Avery. Not if it means you'll have to answer questions about this."

She tried tears. She put her face in her hands and sobbed, and I pushed the sitting room door open and walked past her to the box of tissues on the armoire. I pulled two and held them out to her. She snatched them and held them to her face.

Thorne looked at me and rolled his eyes. Another assumption blown. He was one of the few men who didn't automatically keel over and beg for mercy when faced with the generally foolproof boo-hoo strategem.

"What happened the night Victor died?" I asked.

"I don't *know*," she insisted, shaking her head. She took the tissues away from her face and her eyes were dry, her makeup unsmudged. She dabbed lightly at her face with the tissues, honoring the pretense.

"I wasn't here," she said. "I came home and the house was surrounded by fire trucks. They had already taken Victor's body away."

She took in our neutral expressions and insisted, "Call my friends the Tatmans. I didn't leave the Redwood Room until eleven o'clock. Call the car service. The driver who brought me home saw everything. He offered to drive me back to the Clift so I could stay there instead of here in the house, since it was in shambles."

"Where was Natalie Sunday night?"

"You leave Natalie out of this," she snapped. "She doesn't deserve any more than has already happened to her. She and Victor were making progress after a very rough time. He was taking her to the office with him and she was learning the business. We were sure she was straightening out, that the bad phase was ending. His death has devastated her."

"May we talk to her? Will you call the place where she's staying and tell them to allow it?" I asked, deliberately vague about where or what the place might be.

"Absolutely not. She's lost her father, she's going through withdrawal, she's away from her home and everything she knows. I won't add to the stress she's under."

Sally stared us down. Her face was implacable, her stare granite-hard.

"How was Ellis acquiring stock?" I asked.

"I haven't the faintest idea," she said. But I had shaken her. Fear showed in the creases that appeared on her forehead.

She turned to Thorne. "Did Victor owe you

any money?" she asked. She pronounced "money" as if it were shit on her shoe.

"Not a dime," Thorne answered.

"Leave the keys in the kitchen, please," she said to him. "Your services are no longer required."

She turned and walked from the sitting room into her bedroom. She shut the bedroom door behind her. The lock clicked.

In less than ten minutes Thorne had packed his few clothes into a duffel bag and left his set of keys and Victor's phone on the kitchen island.

He found Lupita wiping down the walls in the dining room and said good bye. She cried real tears and hugged him, reaching up on tiptoe to pat his cheek.

He gave her his full attention, holding his arm around her shoulder until she was finished telling him how much she would miss him and how terrible she felt about the tragedy of this poor family.

He kept murmuring "*si, como no, si, si, yo tambien.*"

Yes, of course, me too.

≂*16*≂

We headed to the Mark Hopkins. Thorne drove. We gave the car keys to the valet, walked into the hotel past the welcoming doorman, and found the elevators. Thorne pressed eighteen.

"What do we do when we get to her room?" I asked him.

"I'll handle it," Thorne said.

On the eighteenth floor, Thorne made me stand ten feet away, in the setback of the next doorway. I could hear him, but I had to peek out to see what was happening.

Thorne knocked and stood to the side, out of sight of the door peephole.

"Who is it?" said the bass voice I had heard the day before.

"Hotel Security with a message for Miss Avery from her mother," Thorne answered.

I heard the door open, then bang against the wall, followed by someone making an *oof* sound. There was a thump, and the floor shook.

"Okay," Thorne called out. I went to the door of 1820 and he was holding a gun, aiming it at a very pissed-off looking man who was curled on his side on the thick tan carpet holding his hands over his abdomen and wheezing. His face was bright red.

From the little I knew about guns, I deduced Thorne was holding a pistol rather than a revolver. It was dark gray and the barrel was straight, without a cylinder for the bullets. Whatever it was, it was making my hair stand up.

Thorne bent down and lifted the man's pant cuffs; he found nothing but dark socks and black leather lace-up shoes. The man was tall—maybe not as tall as Thorne—but bulkier in the middle. He was wearing a dark blue shirt and slacks and a brown leather holster was clipped to his belt. A black sport coat hung on the back of a side chair across the room. Thorne walked over and checked the jacket's pockets, then walked back and stood between me and the man on the floor.

"When you can, get up and sit on the chair." Thorne pointed with the hand that wasn't holding the gun.

We were in a large suite. There was a fireplace surrounded by a down-cushioned sofa and loveseat, a round table with four lyre-backed chairs, and a closed door on the left wall that I assumed led to a bedroom and bath.

It took the man another minute to pull himself to his feet and sit.

Thorne waited until the man looked up at him and was breathing almost normally. He said, "My name is Thorne Ardall. I worked for Victor Avery. Mrs. Avery fired me this morning for looking into her husband's death. We're here to talk to Natalie about it."

No apology for socking the man in the gut and taking his gun. The man looked at Thorne and nodded.

"What's your name?" Thorne asked him.

"Madrone," he said. "Don Madrone."

"Are you keeping her here?"

"That's right. Nobody out and nobody in but room service and the mother."

"Did Sally hire you?"

"Yeah. I do private security. There's three of us taking shifts."

"When's the next guy due on?"

"Noon."

"We're going to talk to her."

"You have the gun," he said.

"I need you to guard him," Thorne said to me without turning his head. "Can you do it? Can you shoot him if he gets up or reaches for the phone? Not threaten to do it—I mean really shoot him."

"No," I said.

"Well, okay," he said.

Thorne thought for a second and said to Madrone, "Get up and go to Natatlie's door slowly, with your hands in the air." He said, "Xana, behind me."

We walked, Thorne behind Don, me behind Thorne, to the door on the left wall.

"Knock," said Thorne. Madrone knocked.

I heard the door open.

"Now sit down," Thorne said, and Madrone backed away and sat. Thorne continued to watch him. I stepped around him and looked at Natalie Avery.

In the doorway, looking at me out of blackened eyes, she had bruises spread like leopard spots across her face. Her dark hair was cropped short and spiked out from her scalp. In her eyes, the brown irises were dull and red capillaries streaked the whites.

She was taller than I, maybe five-ten, and slender in a pullover sweater and jeans. She stood barefoot, with one arm down at her side and the other on the brass doorknob.

"Are you from the police?" she rasped. She held her hand up to her mouth and coughed into it.

"No. I want to ask you about what happened the other night."

"I'm not supposed to talk about it. I promised my mother," she said.

She sounded resigned, like a teenager who has chores to do before she can go out with her friends and have fun, but her eyes shifted away from me and her lean face was grim.

"I'm trying to find out what really happened to Victor Avery," I said.

"He died," she said. She coughed again.

"Could we sit down for a moment? You don't look like you've recovered from the explosion."

She looked mildly curious and moved away from the door and into the bedroom. She stepped over wrinkled clothes she must have worn for the last couple of days, lying in clumps on the carpet. A suitcase heaped with a messy pile of shirts and pants and underwear and shoes gaped on the luggage stand.

We sat at a table and chairs by the window, beyond the unmade bed. "How did you get hurt?" I asked her.

"I'm not supposed to talk," she repeated.

Her threadbare voice made me want to clear my own throat. She sounded like someone whose laryngitis had collided with asthma. Her hand went to her hair and she scrunched a fistful absent-mindedly and pulled her head back and forth. The tips of her fingers were wrapped in flesh-colored bandages.

"Have you seen a doctor?" I asked her.

"Yes. She told me not to talk."

"The doctor or your mother?"

"Both."

"Were you with Victor when the explosion happened?"

"I'm not supposed to talk," she said again, gazing out the window at the bright sunshine and the downtown high rises. It was difficult to tell whether she was drugged or depressed or duplicitous or all three. I thought, what the hell, ask her.

"Did you take the gun from your father's safe?"

"No," she croaked. She waited a moment before continuing. "I didn't know he had one."

But she didn't seem surprised that I had asked her about it. I wasn't sure I believed her. She picked absent-mindedly at a scab on her scalp.

"How long have you been here at the hotel?"

The injustice of her confinement set her off. She glared at me. "I don't know. A couple of days. It feels like forever. There's nothing to do. My mother made the barber come up and cut all my hair off because one side was burned. I look like a dyke. I'm not allowed to talk to anyone. I can't even call my friends. And these guys watching me are all creeps."

Her wounded expression said that the world was not fair. I was not going to tell her how little the world or anyone in it worried about whether things were fair, except perhaps meteorologists.

"Why did you run away from home last year?" I asked.

"That's none of your fucking business," she said. She leaned forward and put her clenched fists in the table and glared. I thought she might take a swing at me. I was now talking to a different creature from the one who had opened the door.

"What happened to Victor Avery two nights ago?" I asked. She had to have been there. There was no other reason for her to look and sound the way she did.

"I don't know what you're talking about," she said. "I was in rehab."

"No, you weren't."

"Go fuck yourself, and that dumb animal who brought you. He's useless for anything else."

She was smiling now. She opened her mouth and flicked her tongue in a rapid pulse, atrociously lewd, against her teeth.

"What caused the explosion?" I asked her.

I had raised my voice. I was frightened. Raising my voice made me feel a little more confident, a little less freaked out by this repellent creature.

"You'll have to ask my dad," she said.

Tears spilled out of her eyes. She coughed and cried and stared out the window, and kept coughing and crying and staring until I slid out of my chair and backed out of the room. I watched her as I backed up. I didn't bother to bring her a box of tissues. Let the Avery women get their own damn tissues from now on.

I shut the door to Natalie's room behind me.

"Mother*fuck*er!" she shouted in a grating, scraped voice.

Something heavy, maybe a chair, slammed against the wall and fell to the floor in her room.

Thorne and Don Madrone looked up at me and I shrugged. They were regaling each other with stories about people they had bodyguarded, only they called it "personal security." They wrapped up their chat and stood. They were cordial with each other, but Thorne kept his distance and held the gun steady, pointed at Natalie's minder.

Thorne apologized for decking Don, and Don said he wouldn't say anything to anybody about our visit if Natalie didn't because it was a little embarrassing how Thorne had gotten the drop on him, and I said Natalie might not blab but you never know, she seemed a little hard to gauge, and Don shook his head and put his hand alongside his mouth and whispered she was a piece of work all right, and Thorne said he'd leave the pistol on the floor by the elevator once we were on the way down, and Don said that he understood, you could never be too careful.

In the elevator I said, "That girl was very scary. Also, given the evidence so far today, I must conclude that this blue jacket is not in the least conversational. Not at all like my red leather one."

Thorne told me Madrone had indicated that in his opinion Natalie was not a very nice person, but he had not provided specifics because that would be unprofessional.

We overtipped the parking valet.

≈17≈

I called information and between us we found our way to the number for Bayside Steel, Bix Bonebreak's metal fabricating company. I called and, miracle of miracles, reached an actual person at the main number.

"Good morning, Bayside Steel, Hannah speaking. How may I help you?"

Amazing. Had these folks never heard of automated answering systems? They could be producing countless infuriated customers each day, just like every other business.

"This is Xana Bard," I said. "I'm calling Bix Bonebreak, please."

"I'll transfer you."

"Jonelle Wolfen," someone answered. Another actual human person answering her own phone. I was stupefied. Hers was a low, straightforward voice, politely confident.

I told her my name and that I was a friend of DeDe's, and asked whether it would be possible to speak to Mr. Bonebreak at his convenience.

"Let me see what's going on with his schedule," she said, and put me on hold. I did not hear the easy listening version of "Proud Mary," nor did some hyped-up announcer tell me how I could buy more scrap metal.

"Bonebreak." Deep, with an edge that could cut ingot.

"Mr. Bonebreak, my name is Xana Bard, and..."

"Jonelle told me who you are. She said you know DeDe."

"Yes, sir, I do."

"What do you want?" he asked. He wasn't outright rude, but his tone made it clear that I had maybe four seconds to explain myself before he hung up.

"I'd like to see you as soon as you can manage to make time for it. It's about Victor Avery."

There was silence. I waited.

"Do you know where my office is?" he asked.

"On Folsom between 17th and 18th Streets," I said.

"Tell the guard who you are and he'll find me." There was a click and I was the only one left on the line.

א א א

Bayside Steel takes up an entire city block in the Mission District. The building is three stories tall, with a utilitarian exterior of corrugated steel and no windows. The company name is painted in big, plain blue letters above the entrance.

We could hear the semi engines grumbling in the loading dock around the corner, and the screech of stamping presses and extruding machinery muted only slightly by the shell of the building.

When Thorne and I walked in the guard stood up behind the counter in front of us.

He looked to be in his sixties, with a thick crop of wavy grey hair cut short around his long ears. His hard, intelligent blue eyes assessed us carefully as we walked up to the high counter. He wore a tan shirt with no name tag, black polished cotton pants with a wide leather belt that supported a holster on one hip holding a cell phone and another holster on the other hip with a gun snapped into it.

He tilted his florid face with its beak of a nose at an angle as if he were sniffing out how much of a threat we posed to him. Me, not too much apparently, but when the guard looked at Thorne he lifted his hands up from his sides and spread his open fingers out on his belt above the holsters.

"Miss Bard?" he said to me. I nodded.

"May I know your name, please?" I asked.

He thought about it for a few seconds.

"Henry," he said finally.

"And this gentleman?" he asked, still looking at me but nodding at Thorne.

"Ardall," said Thorne. "I'm with her."

Henry and Thorne stared at each other. I counted to five and then gave up. They stared some more, in that meaningful but silent way men have that I don't really get, but that makes perfect sense to them.

"Sit tight for a second," Henry said at last, and pulled a key ring from a desk drawer. He unlocked a steel door behind his desk and disappeared through it, the shop sounds buffeting us until the door hissed shut behind him.

We waited less than a minute for him to return. He pointed a thick index finger first at me, then at Thorne.

"You come with me. He stays here."

"No," I said.

"No," Thorne said at the same time.

"The boss said so," Henry argued.

"But not until you made your recommendation," I said. "And who can blame you? The thing is, he's my partner in this conversation. I'd appreciate it if you would explain that to Mr. Bonebreak."

He stared at Thorne some more, then looked at me, then turned and went back through the steel door. It took longer for him to come back this time.

"Okay," he said. "You packing?" he asked Thorne.

Thorne shook his head no, holding up his arms and rotating once in place for Henry's benefit.

"C'mon then," Henry said, unlocking the door again, and we walked into the roar of the mill.

We climbed up a metal grid staircase open on the sides. I was hugging the handrail, Henry huffed a little as we neared the top, and Thorne was taking the stairs two at a time. Below us sparks sprayed out from the machine welder down on the shop floor. Henry opened a door at the top of the stairs for us and stood out of our way as we walked in. He closed the door behind us and we heard his footsteps clanging on the metal stairs as he marched back down.

We were in an office, twelve by fourteen feet or so, with a desk on the left and two brown leather chairs against the wall on the right. There was a door straight ahead of us.

Seated in the leather chairs were two men, both wearing suits, one suit pesto green and other the color of mustard that's dried around the mouth of the jar. Both suits were ill-fitting over the many muscles each man was swollen with, and both men wore loosened but hideous ties looped through their spread collars. They stood up and stared at Thorne. He stared back. I allowed them to stare without interruption, and took charge of the next required activity on our schedule, turning to the woman who must be Jonelle.

"Hello," I said, to the hummingbird of a woman seated at the desk, peering at us over her tortoise shell reading glasses. She wore a carefully ironed white blouse open one button at the top, with Mrs. Cleaver pearls around her neck. She looked at me, but not for long, because she saw Thorne.

She rested her pencil eraser-down on the papers she had been reading, sat up straighter, smiled at him, took off her glasses, stood up, put down the pencil, smoothed her skirt over her hips, walked around her desk to the door across from us, opened it, and said "Go on in."

As petite as she was, she managed to block the way enough that I could just get past her by turning sideways a little, but Thorne would have to brush against her to get through. Her eyes stayed on Thorne as we walked across the tightly woven industrial carpet and through the door.

"Thank you," he said, looming over her. The top of her head was just about as high as the bottom of his rib cage.

"Any time," Jonelle said, leaning toward the part of him that seemed to interest her the most as he slid past.

We found ourselves in a spacious office holding a colossal man seated behind an aircraft carrier deck of a desk. Bix Bonebreak stood up, and then kept standing up until he dwarfed everything in the room except his desk and the man behind me. Bonebreak was as tall as Thorne–

easily six and a half feet–and as broad and hard as the plank of a monastery refectory table. He had gray eyes, a little hooded under dark bristling eyebrows and a wide forehead as corrugated as the side of his building.

He was wearing a light blue and white striped dress shirt with French cuffs, charcoal suit pants held up by a black suspenders, and a somber gray tie with a tidy pattern. The suit jacket hung on a wooden hanger on the coat tree in the corner.

Bonebreak looked prosperous and capable and strong. He was certainly intimidating, but also a little wary. He wasn't scowling at me, but he wasn't smiling either. He just seemed to be waiting, not very patiently, for whatever was about to happen.

So I held out my hand and said, "Thank you for agreeing to see me, Mr. Bonebreak. I'm Xana Bard and this is my associate Thorne Ardall."

He took my hand and it disappeared up to the wrist in his. He nodded at Thorne as he did it. Thorne nodded back. Unlike most big men, Bonebreak didn't pulverize my fingers; he matched the pressure I used, and the calluses of his palm and the heat of his dry skin made my hand feel like it was resting on a sunbaked boulder.

"It's Bix," he said. "Sit." He pointed at the two wooden chairs in front of his desk. They looked like old library chairs, unbreakable and curved and oddly comfortable, but in this office not intended for anyone to sit in them for very long.

Convicts used to make chairs like that during their stint at San Quentin.

I sat. Thorne backed up to the wall next to the door and leaned against it, crossing his arms. A little of the man-staring thing happened between the two men, and then Bix shrugged, sat down, and looked at me.

This was not a man with whom one exchanged small talk, it seemed to me, so I said, "I'm here to ask you about Victor Avery. Thorne worked for him, and Mrs. Avery asked us to do what we could to learn about his death."

It was a small enough lie that I forgave myself for saying it.

"What does this have to do with DeDe?" Bix asked.

"Nothing, really," I answered. "I saw her last night after the symphony and your name came up as someone who was interested in buying Victor's company."

He looked at me for a few seconds, and then his face darkened to a deep red. His voice changed from a calm bass rumble to a deep ripsaw rasp.

"Wait a minute. I know who you are–you're that meddling bitch Louisa Bard's daughter."

When he saw how shocked I was he caught himself, the color fleeing from his face.

"I'm sorry. You seem like you have some manners and it's not your fault who your mother is. But I thought you were here because DeDe asked you to come see me."

He shook his big head and covered his eyes with his dinner plate of a hand.

Well, there it was. DeDe turned fuchsia when his name was mentioned, my mother's voice sharpened under the same circumstances, and Bix covered his eyes when he found out DeDe hadn't asked me to come.

"DeDe's a widow now, you know," I said.

"Yeah, but I'm married," he said, looking back up at me, "and my wife's a good woman. And my kids are good kids."

He shook his head like a horse shaking off flies. We sat quietly, the sounds of the factory faint in the fluorescent-lit office. He reached a decision and looked back at me.

"Your mother wagged her finger at me one time and accused me of being uncouth. That's bullshit," he snarled at me. "I'm *lousy* with couth."

I couldn't help it. I laughed out loud and then slapped my hand over my mouth and lifted my eyebrows at him in surprise.

A roar of laughter erupted from Bix Bonebreak, and we both laughed very hard, and then we sat back in our chairs and gazed at each other, smiling all the way up past our eyes.

"Listen," he said, "You want to know about Victor, I'll tell you. I was buying Victor's company because he wanted to sell it, and it made good business sense. He was having some family problems, he told me, and wanted out. I'm sure your mother's told you things about me, and they're probably not all lies, either. But I didn't kill Victor, and my guys didn't kill Victor, and I don't know who killed Victor, so if that's what you came here to find out, you've found out."

He was a tough scary man, as unbreakable as one of the girders his mill hands forged, but he was like my Dad: his word was his bond and when he told you something you could believe him.

"Thank you for seeing me on such short notice," I said, and stood up. He nodded and we shook hands again. He waved goodbye to Thorne.

I looked back at him as I went out. Bix Bonebreak was standing, looking down at his desk, hands on his hips, seeing nothing.

≈18≈

I asked Thorne to drive to Ocean Beach. We parked facing out to sea in a lot on top of the dunes at the end of Sloat Boulevard, past the San Francisco Zoo and the water treatment plant.

Ten-foot waves pound against seven miles of beach along the western shore of the City. The water is fifty-something degrees. Rows of foam-edged breakers were pounding ka-whump onto the beach.

From a safe distance, the water and the light and the sound of the Pacific are my restoratives. I come here, I tell people, to confer with this alternate Doctor P. One Doctor P. charges a small fortune per hour and requires an appointment; the other Doctor P. costs zip and is on duty twenty-four-seven, such a deal.

Sitting in the warm car, protected from the cold wind flattening the dune grass, staring at the blue-gray surf, I thought about how poorly things were going. I worked on re-establishing my equilibrium.

We were into the full Fool Card experience with the Averys. Unpredictable and unsafe things were happening and there was no telling what would come next. Now I was literally sitting on the edge of a precipice, a wolf-man at my side, striding fearlessly into an unknown and potentially dangerous future.

I tell people who have the Fool Card in their reading to hang on and be patient. The card represents a life experience that picks you up the way a mother cat carries her kitten. The kitten goes wherever the cat takes it, with no control over what's going on, and can only hope to be put down gently after the ride. The implicit lesson is that the mother's intent is to act as protector and guardian, and we need to trust that the experience will end for the best.

And so I was trying to trust the experience. I was working on having faith that the situation with Thorne and the Averys, and my involvement with them all, would end for the best. I thought "for the best" might require a liberal interpretation, and the Averys might not agree with me about what was best.

Amicably silent, Thorne and I sat. He didn't ask me why I wanted to come here, and I didn't explain. I breathed in and out and in and out and watched the water. It took a while, and then I found equilibrium. With equilibrium came a new intuition.

"I need to talk to my sister," I said, and I pulled out my cell phone and called Yolanda.

Yolanda is a sister but not a sibling. She's African-American, of unspecified age, and I met her when I was singing in a gospel choir for a while. She lives across the Bay in Oakland and she's a tax attorney. She's also one of the few friends I have who lives someplace I can drive to and visit without it taking a week or more. I have a knack for long-distance friendships, more so than for local ones.

"Hey there, YoYo," I said when she answered her phone.

"Hey yourself, Triple Ex. How you doin', girl?"

"Good, good. I have a question for you. Do you have a minute?"

"It's high tax season, girlfriend, so ask me fast and don't get your feelings all hurt if I answer you back just as fast."

"Deal. I need to know what options rich people with children have for sheltering wealth, particularly wealth in the form of shares in the parent's publicly held company."

"Oh, sure, nothing complicated in the answer to that one. How do rich people hide their money? As many ways as there are rich people is how.

You're gonna have to tell me more about the family if I'm supposed to come up with something specific."

I told her about the Averys, and she gave me the most likely answer, and I said thank you and got off the phone. I was confident now that I knew what had happened. I told Thorne and he agreed with me.

Ellis could tell us if I was right. We drove down the peninsula, up his driveway through the ugly, smelly trees, and parked in front of the glass house.

א א א

Ellis joined the parade of people who so far today hadn't wanted to let us in. Thorne loomed over him and Ellis changed his mind.

I sat down on one leather bench and Ellis sat on the other. He didn't bother to offer us refreshments. Thorne stood against the plate glass wall behind Ellis and monitored the conversation. There was a cooler on the kitchen counter. A suitcase stood at the bottom of the stairs.

"Are you taking a trip? Perhaps a return to your family?" I asked him.

"I told you, the deal is off. I can't proceed now that Victor is gone, so I'm going home."

"Tell us about your relationship with Natalie Avery," I said.

"My niece," he said, and laughed sarcastically.

"Your daughter," I corrected him.

Ellis tilted his head gave me a speculative look. "I didn't think Sally would tell anyone."

"She didn't. How long have you known?" I asked.

I could see Ellis mulling over what he should or shouldn't admit to me. When he looked up I saw a man who wanted to tell me his story, and who wouldn't be stopped once he started.

"I recognized Sally when I first got into town and dropped in at Victor's house. I met her a long time ago, and I was drunk that night, but you'd have to be blind or dead to forget a woman who looked like her."

"It was eighteen years ago."

"It was the day I got kicked out of Princeton. I remember everything that happened that day. I went out to get drunk with my friends as a fare-well. She was working as the hostess in this old Italian place outside Trenton. We were all kidding around with her, trying to pick her up, until her father comes over and tells us to keep it down or he'll ask us to leave."

"Why did she end up going out with you?"

"I wrote her a note on a cocktail napkin, for Chrissake, and handed it to her as we walked out." He laughed again. "I never thought she'd show up, but there she was, at this townie bar on the Post Road back to campus. Sullivan's, Mulligan's, Hoolihan's, something like that. I was nicer-looking back then," he said, smoothing his thin hair.

"Were your friends still with you?"

"Are you kidding? Why would I bring them along? I dropped them off at the fraternity house. I was supposed to catch a plane the next morning, and I planned to stay out all night and stay drunk."

"Did you know how old she was?"

"No. How old was she?"

"Seventeen."

He put his head down on his hands and laughed again, this time more rueful than sarcastic.

"No wonder," he said.

"No wonder what?"

"She was incredible looking, you know? Working at that restaurant where guys must have been hitting on her right and left. She told me she'd only just started working the front. She said she went to Catholic school and her parents kept a pretty tight lid on her, didn't let her date. I figured that must be the only reason she agreed to come out with me, you know? She was cutting loose a little."

"And?"

"Look, she wasn't the first girl who wanted me to help her get past being a virgin." Apparently my expression was doubtful. He smiled then, like he could help me out as well if I only had the sense to take him up on it.

"Did she say that?"

I was trying to keep my tone under control,

but I heard a little edge slide in there.

"No, it wasn't what she said. It's what she did after we had a couple of beers. She nearly threw me into the back seat."

"And then later that night you drove up on the dean's lawn?"

"I took her home and told her I'd see her at her dad's restaurant, and then I went back to the road house and kept drinking until they kicked me out. I had a six-pack in the car and I kept drinking until I drank 'em all, and the next thing I remember, some lawyer my dad called is bailing me out of jail and I'm on a plane to San Francisco."

"Only to be shipped off to Europe."

"My dad had friends there, people who were customers and over the years had become friends. They knew my grandfather, even."

"So you never knew you'd gotten Sally pregnant?"

"I never saw her again until three months ago when I rang the doorbell at the house. And after that Victor wouldn't ever meet me at the house. It was always hotels or restaurants or, lately, here at this place." He gestured around himself at the glass walls.

"Where have you been for all these years?" I asked.

"Everywhere. Nowhere." He shook his head.

"Why did you come back?"

"Victor opened a new plant in Biloxi. I saw an

article in the paper about it. I was working for a shrimper, mending and storing nets, and the boss left the newspaper lying around one morning." He shrugged his shoulders, as if he'd explained himself adequately.

"But you'd been gone for years. Why come back now?"

"I read the article, and there was a picture of Victor all suited up, the mayor shaking his hand. It pissed me off.

"Everybody was always holding him up as such a fucking great example. Victor this, Victor that, just nonstop Victor. 'Why don't you get good grades like Victor? Why don't you work hard like Victor?' It was fucking annoying, especially when I was the one who knew the Victor nobody else did. Just me. Lucky me, the baby brother. I'm the one Victor used to grab and punch in the arm when no one was looking. Anytime I complained my dad would tell me not to tattle and my mother would kiss me and tell him, 'Now, Victor, that's not nice.' Fat lot of good that did."

"I have two older brothers. It sounds like the way brothers act with each other."

"It was more than that. When nobody was around he used to taunt me that Dad would give him everything and I'd get nothing. That he was Dad's favorite and I was going to be an orphan. That anybody could see I didn't have what it took. Oh, everybody was always patting him on the head, telling him what a little prince he was, and he knew exactly how to suck up to the grown-ups. Everybody was always saying 'Poor Ellis' when they looked at me. He knew exactly what he was doing. To this day, everybody thinks Victor was a great guy, Mr. Integrity. Well, I grew up with him, and he was a cruel bastard, is what he was." Ellis's face had twisted with resentment as he talked.

"You hadn't seen him in years," I said. "Perhaps during that time he remade himself into the person everyone believed him to be."

"I don't think so. Not for a minute." Ellis was adamant, shaking his head no.

"So you come back here, and the first person you see is Sally. Then what?"

He laughed out loud, a nasty triumphant *Hah!* "I knew I had him!" he gloated. "Sally tried to get me out of there, but I threatened to tell Victor. I knew right away she couldn't have told Victor about me. He'd never have touched her if he'd known. And she had to have known Victor was my brother when she married him. Back then I told her my name, and that my family was from San Francisco. Plus Victor and I look like brothers. And then Natalie walked in. I thought Sally was going to pass out. She introduced me to Natalie as Uncle Ellis, but I could tell she knew I had figured things out."

"Mr. Avery, who's been selling you shares in Avery Chemical? Who's been financing your takeover attempt?"

"Victor!"   He lifted his feet off the floor and rocked from side to side, laughing and clapping his hands together. "That son of a bitch! Oh, it's been great. So fucking great."

I remembered what Yolanda had told me. "He split his majority sharehold didn't he? Some shares to Sally, some to Natalie as part of the uniform gift to minors tax shelter, right? He set aside shares every year and put them in a trust while she was growing up, to pay for college tuition when the time came."

"That's right," Ellis said. "Last year I got a phone call from this girl who says she's my daughter. Turns out Natalie had been doing what teenage girls do, rummaging in her mother's jewelry box, and she found her birth certificate hidden in there. She saw my name and asked Sally about it. Sally tried to say it was an error, but Natalie didn't buy it."

"Is that why Natalie ran away from home?"

"That's what she told me. She said she was furious at her mother, furious at both of them for never once mentioning that I existed. She said she was determined to find her 'real' father."

"How did she track you down?"

"How do you find anybody nowadays? The Internet. My phone number is listed, and she called me to make sure who I was and then got on a bus to Mississippi."

"Does she know about your plan to take over the company?" I asked.

"She *thought* of it! I told her about the real Victor. She saw how my family lives, how hard my wife and I work, and she said she had all this stock that Victor had put away for her. She said we could take over the company and Victor wouldn't know what hit him. Even if it didn't work, I could at least get a fair share of what I was entitled to."

"Once you had the plan worked out, she called her Dad and said she was ready to come back home?"

"Yeah. I drove her to New Orleans and she called him, and Victor flew in and got her. We gave it a couple of months and then I showed up and we started the ball rolling."

"But how does it work?" I asked. "She's still a minor. She can't sell her shares from the trust."

"But Sally could. Sally's a co-trustee. She sold me her own shares as well, and month by month she liquidated the trust. Sally gave me the proceeds from what she sold and I bought Avery shares with the money.

"We had to do it over time," he went on, "because I needed the payout from one sale to buy the shares from the next sale. In another two months I'd have had thirty percent of the company. I forced Sally to sell some other assets as well, stocks and jewelry, so I could buy any other Avery shares that came available. We tried to get that faggot CFO to help. Natalie had overheard Victor talking about the problems the guy was having. Nothing really came of that but some inside information, but it didn't really matter by then. The whole thing was *beautiful*." He gave an exultant, cackling laugh. "A real masterpiece. Victor's even paying for this house! And my rental car!"

"But how could Victor not have known?"

It took all my self-control and some more that I borrowed by looking up at Thorne's stoic face to keep myself from spitting at this repulsive man. I wanted to find out what had happened more than I wanted to indulge my disgust, and I choked back the scorn I felt, forcing my tone to remain neutral.

"Natalie used her computer to produce dummy statements. She took the real ones, the accurate ones that came in the mail, and replaced them with the phonies. Victor never knew what was going on. He was never going to know what hit him."

"But he would have found out in the end. He would have confronted Sally and it all would have come out." I couldn't believe Sally had done something so stupid. "How was she hoping to survive it when Victor discovered what all of you had done?"

"That I don't know, and I don't care either. Victor would have divorced her, that's for sure. But he never would have sent her to jail, not him. He was that crazy about her. Even if all of it wound up in the middle of a bunch of flying lawsuits, he still would have been ruined. Anyway, California is a community property state. No matter what Sally did, she gets half of everything unless he sends her to jail for fraud. Maybe getting half of what was left was enough for her. Or maybe she thought she'd figure something out along the way, hold back the tide somehow. People tend to think they'll figure something out before the collapse crushes them."

I was shaking my head. I hadn't realized I was doing it. Ellis apparently thought I disapproved. But then I did disapprove.

"You know," he said, "she married him knowing he was my brother. It's not like she couldn't anticipate that I would show up someday. And she's not the first person to panic and do something crazy rather than face the music. She didn't want to tell Victor until she absolutely had to. Maybe she thought she could convince him it was all lies. Who knows?"

"But now it stops."

"Now it stops," he agreed, his smile fading. "She doesn't have to sell me anything anymore because there's no Victor to keep secrets from now."

He put his hands down on his knees. "What the hell. I've got a lot more than I started with. I can sell off the shares I own and live well for a lot of years. I can live the way I was brought up to instead of the way I've had to."

He looked down at his hands. They were callused and scarred. The tip of his right index finger was missing. Not a rich man's hands.

"Do you think Sally killed him to stop all this from coming to light?" I asked.

He didn't hesitate. He looked directly at me and said "No."

"You were there the night he was killed, yes?"

This time he hesitated. Then, "Yes."

Thorne spoke up. "You came in by the door to the library."

Ellis turned to face Thorne. "That's right."

"How did you get through the gate?" Thorne asked.

"With the code."

"How did you know the code?"

Ellis shrugged. He wasn't going to say how he knew the code.

"Natalie," Thorne said. "She knew. And she took the video."

"Yes. I didn't know there were security cameras. She said we had to take the footage for that night before you came back downstairs."

"Natalie was with you," I said. "The two of you drove away in the Jaguar."

Ellis turned around to me again and laughed. "No. I had my own car."

"Natalie drove the Jag."

"You are fucking scary," he said. "How do you know so much about all this?"

"Natalie's damaged face and hair and voice. Sally has her stashed at the Mark Hopkins."

"I know. I talked to Sally yesterday. But how did you manage to see Natalie?"

That wasn't important for him to know, I decided. "When I asked Natalie what happened, she said I would have to ask her dad. She didn't mean Victor—he was dead. She meant you, didn't she?"

"She said that? She called me her dad?"

He was startled. I couldn't tell if he was pleased or not.

"How did you survive the explosion?" I went on, ignoring his questions. "Were you in the library too?"

"I was." Ellis said. "Natalie and Victor and I, we were all in there. Sally called me earlier in the day and said Natalie was using again and had flipped out. She said Natalie was stealing ether from the plant and freebasing.

"She told me they'd had a huge fight, and Natalie stormed out of the house to stay at a friend's. She said Natalie was planning to confront Victor about 'stealing the company from her real dad' when he got home that evening. Sally begged me to stop her. She said that Natalie was going to tell Victor and wreck everything, and that if I wanted to get control of Avery Chemical, I would have to calm Natalie down."

"Why did Sally go to dinner at the Clift? Why didn't she stay home?" I asked.

"She already had the dinner thing planned. I told her I'd go to the friend's house and handle Natalie. I told Sally it would only make things more complicated if she were with me, that Natalie would act up if her mother was there."

"So what went wrong?"

"Sally had no idea I was going to pick Natalie up at her friend's house and take her home to see Victor. When we saw the light in the library, we walked around to the garden. Natalie knew Mr. Muscles-for-Brains back there"—he aimed his thumb over his shoulder at Thorne—"wouldn't let me in to see Victor, so we snuck in by the library door."

Thorne had crossed his arms over his chest, biceps prominent, and his feet were shoulder width apart, acting out the nickname. He hadn't taken his eyes off Ellis; his stare was focused and steady.

"You thought it'd be fun to watch Natalie rip into her devoted dad," I said. "Adoptive dad."

He smirked. "Guilty," he admitted. "Can you blame me? I finally get a chance to demolish that asshole's smug attitude, I'm not going to let it pass.

"Natalie was carrying that cooler over there." Ellis pointed to the one on the counter. "I thought it was sodas or something," he went on. "She carried it into the library and put it on that big partner desk of my dad's. That desk was Victor's pride and joy.

"He was standing over by the fire," he continued. "He always loved to have fires in that fireplace. We learned that from Dad. The library always smelled of applewood smoke. More than the books or the leather chairs or the lavender furniture polish Lupita uses.

"When we were little Lupita would clean out that fireplace every day and put in fresh logs and kindling and newspaper. I always liked helping with that." He was staring into space, remembering.

I pulled him back into the present. "What happened when you and Natalie walked in?"

"Victor was pissed when he saw me with her. He asked Natalie what she thought she was doing bringing me to the house, and she just uncorked. She started yelling at him, telling him he'd lied to her all these years, that her mother had lied to her all these years, that I was her real father."

"And?"

"It was everything I could have hoped for."

Ellis's eyes blazed with the venom he felt toward his dead brother. "Victor could not have been more stunned. He didn't say a thing, kept staring at her and me. You could see him figuring things out." Ellis paused and looked down at his hands. He spread out his fingers and flexed them. "And then he did the most peculiar thing."

"What?"

"He turned away from us and looked at a picture of Dad and Mom on the bookshelf. He looked at that picture for what seemed like forever." Ellis thought for a moment. "Huh," he went on. "Maybe Victor thought Dad would speak up from the photograph and tell him what the hell he should do next."

"What did he do?"

"Not him, he didn't do anything. It was *Natalie*. She went *berserk*. She yelled at him not to turn his back on her, and she reached across the desk and opened the cooler. She grabbed a canister and threw it into the fireplace."

"It was ether."

"Yeah. What a lunatic thing to do. It was a sixteen-ounce can. Victor had been taking her down to the plant with him to learn the business. She had friends who needed ether to manufacture drugs, so she helped herself one time. So stupid. That stuff is incredibly unsafe unless you store it correctly. She had dry ice in there with it, so she had to know what would happen if she tossed it into the fire. The canister was so cold I think it pulled some skin off of her fingers when she threw it."

"What did Victor do?"

"He grabbed the fireplace tongs and tried to pull it out of there. It exploded before he could grab it." Ellis slumped and put his hands up over his face.

"Why weren't you hurt?" I asked.

He put his hands down. "I ducked down behind the desk as soon as I realized what it was Natalie had thrown. I grabbed the cooler, grabbed Natalie's arm, and dragged her down behind the desk with me. She almost made it, but the blast caught her face before she was all the way down. Her hair caught fire and I had to smother it with my jacket to put it out."

Thorne moved to the kitchen counter, continuing to watch Ellis as he went, and lifted the lid off the cooler. He turned it upside down so I could see it was empty. He put it down again and saw something next to it, by the telephone. He held it up: a turquoise pen. The turquoise pen of the threatening note left in my mailbox.

Ellis hadn't seen Thorne do any of this. If I hadn't watched Thorne move, I wouldn't have known he was doing it either. He was as silent as the dust motes that floated in the sunbeams passing through the glass walls. He moved back behind Ellis.

"Natalie has a cough. Why don't you?"

"I knew to hold my breath until we got outside. Ether is extremely caustic."

"Why did you pull her to safety?" I asked. "With Natalie out of the picture you could dominate the company."

"I suppose." Ellis laughed again and shook his head. "I just grabbed her." He thought about it for a minute. "Do you have any kids?" he asked me.

"No," I said.

"I do. A boy and a girl, seven and five. My wife is somebody the Avery family would never have countenanced, and my kids go to public school. But now Natalie's another daughter," he said. "She's my daughter, and I grabbed her and pulled her down behind the desk." He shrugged.

"Are you saying you set this whole scam up because of your family?"

"I did all this because I could," he said, a note of pride in his voice. "Yes, it will help my family, but it was also to pay my parents back for their unfairness, and to pay Victor back for the misery he caused me."

"Not only Victor. You've ruined Sally's life as well. And Natalie—well, the police are going to have to be involved."

"It was an accident."

I shook my head no.

"It was anything but. It was either first- or second-degree murder, if I know my murders. You're relatively safe, since all you're on the hook for is leaving the scene of a crime, aiding and abetting, material witness, extortion, fraud, whatever. But get yourself the right lawyer and I'll bet there's a deal in your future, should you choose to accept it. You can turn Natalie and Sally in and keep your thirty percent of the shares. How much is that worth, do you think? Some millions, no doubt. But wait, you've decided to go home to Biloxi. You think you can skate on this whole thing!"

"Natalie is only seventeen," he protested.

"In this state, if a crime is outrageous enough, they try three-year-olds as adults. Your daughter has to come forward and hope that, like rich people the world over, she can hire an expensive-enough attorney to get her acquitted."

He thought about it, his gaze inward.

"The fire tongs slammed across Victor and cut him apart. After everything exploded, Natalie was crying like nothing I've ever heard. Her face was all black and red, her hair was fried, and she was wailing out loud. I could barely hear her, though. I couldn't hear much of anything for hours. I have nightmares about it. She grew up thinking Victor was her father, and she saw him just about split in half, blood everywhere. I can't imagine what she's going through."

I couldn't muster much sympathy for either of them.

"Who took Victor's gun?" I asked.

"She did. She opened the safe in the cabinet behind his desk and grabbed the gun and a full bullet clip. I dragged her out the same door we came in, but she fought me until she got loose, and then ran down to the garage. I guessed it wouldn't be long before Hercules here showed up, so as soon as I saw that Natalie was in the Jaguar I got into my own car and got the hell out of there."

"Did you try to stay with her, follow her, do anything about her?" I asked.

"No," he said. "I saw the Porsche coming after her and I got out of the way."

"You were driving a black Lexus?" Thorne spoke up.

Ellis turned to face him. "Yes."

"You turned right on Clement."

"If you say so," Ellis said. He turned back to me. "You two are quite the tag team," he said. "What are you, anyway? Lovers? Partners? Brother and sister?"

I looked up at Thorne and he looked down at me.

"Uncategorizable," Thorne said.

I smiled a little smile and nodded.

"And after that you drove down here?" I asked Ellis, ready to wrap this conversation up.

"I drove down here."

"What have you been doing since? Have you talked to Sally or Natalie since yesterday?"

"No," he answered. "What would I say to them now?"

If he couldn't figure that out, I had no suggestions for him.

≈19≈

"Whew," I said, when Thorne had driven us onto the two-lane road leading down the hill away from the glass house.

"Yep," he said.

I looked out at the trees alongside the road. The live oaks hugged the culverts with their dark evergreen leaves and contorted bark-brown trunks. They were timeless and sturdy, and suddenly I was in tears, unzipping my purse and rooting around for a Kleenex.

Thorne said nothing. He drove us smoothly down the hill to open grassland awash with sunlight. He pulled over and put the car in park. I blew my nose and leaned back in the leather seat.

"Do you mind if I open the sunroof?" I asked him.

He reached up and pressed a button above the mirror. The upholstered panel and sunroof glass went gliding open until I could feel the cool breeze in my hair and the warm sunlight on my face. I took in a deep breath and let it out slowly.

"I miss my father," I said, thinking about the three fathers in the Avery family.

"Where is he?" Thorne said.

"He died years ago."

"Were you close?"

"In a way that isn't easy to describe," I said. A memory surfaced. "He taught me to dance when I was little. He would put records on the stereo—big band and Dixieland and swing—and the two of us would dance all around the front hall. I don't think I've ever been so happy since. It stayed with me, you know? The joy of it. That he really saw me, that he recognized the real me, when we danced together.

"By the time I was ten or eleven he was too busy to dance anymore. He was traveling all the time, making money. Big pots of money. And then he moved out and disappeared from our lives when I was a teenager. I thought he didn't love me anymore. I couldn't take it in that he was leaving my mother, not me."

I paused and thought. "I didn't find out until later that she blocked him from having any contact with all of us. And then he was gone."

"Do you have brothers or sisters?"

"Two older brothers and two younger sisters. I'm in the middle, the oldest girl."

"Did the others dance too?"

"I don't remember that they did. They were off doing other things, is my recollection. It was just my Dad and me, and Bennie Goodman and Pete Fountain and Artie Shaw. Anytime I hear a clarinet now I think of Dad."

"You were lucky."

"After he died, after the funeral, I had a fight with my mother over it. I told her I missed him, and that I missed dancing with him. That dancing together was when I knew he loved me. She said he didn't love me, that he was incapable of loving anyone."

"What?!"

"It was one of the only times I've taken her on. For once, I found words. 'In the first place,' I said, 'I know he loved me. I am absolutely certain of it, and nothing you say will ever convince me otherwise. But meanwhile, what mother tells a child her father doesn't love her? How can you possibly think it's okay to say something like that to me?'

"I got it that she never felt loved," I went on, "and I felt sorry for her, but keep that shit to yourself, lady, was what I was thinking. She apologized. She knew she was out of line. But there's been—oh, call it 'unease' between us ever since."

"Why did she say it?"

"Jesus, Thorne, I'm not smart enough to figure it out. It's just wrong, you know?"

He nodded.

"Anyway, I'm trying to fathom what was going on with Natalie when she discovered that her two dads were brothers and they were at war with each other. That her mother had conceived her with one and married the other.

"Natalie thought Victor knew about it and had kept it a secret," I went on. "But Ellis says Victor was shocked when Natalie told him, and he said that Sally insisted Victor didn't know. I think dads and daughters everywhere make a connection that causes chaos when it's tampered with, the same way mothers and sons do."

"Sigmund, meet Xana. Xana, Sigmund."

"Sigmund cribbed from Sophocles and Euripides. He loses points for plagiarism."

"You didn't ask about the threat in the mailbox." Thorne said, starting up the car. We drove along Skyline Boulevard, headed to the beach and the maritime Dr. P.

"Why bother? You showed me the turquoise pen, so we know he wrote it. Ellis is leaving town millions of dollars to the better, so the threat is empty now."

"Not if you plan to tell the police."

"Ellis won't come after me. No one can prove he blackmailed Sally, and Natalie won't blame him for anything. It's Natalie and Sally who are in real trouble, although Sally was a co-trustee and it's legally her own money she gave away, and to a family member at that.

"One would imagine she and Natalie are Victor's principal heirs. But if Natalie is convicted of causing Victor's death, she can't inherit and it all goes to Sally. Meanwhile Sally's been protecting Natalie, but she has to realize she can't do that forever. I don't envy those two the decisions they're going to have to make."

"I don't think this is over yet. We know what happened, but that doesn't mean we're safe."

He turned out to be right, and I turned out to be wrong. I found out soon enough how fortunate I was that he was ready to be right. The readiness is all.

≈20≈

At the East-West Café, Rose brought us Minty Chix in Let Us Cups and we shared. Rolling up the grilled chicken in the lettuce leaves, we ate them like soft tacos as we debated our next move.

I voted for giving Sally one last chance to do the right thing and turn Natalie in. It was what people in my mother's set were supposed to do, after which you counted on your chums the judges and the custom-suit-clad lawyers to keep you from doing any actual jail time. For all we knew, the police had figured out exactly what we had figured out, and were trying to track Natalie down as we spoke.

Thorne pointed out that the police did not wear clothing as conversational as mine, so people they questioned were less likely to unburden themselves of incriminating facts unless they had some form of confessional Tourette's.

He also pointed out that Sally was excluded from the Avery crowd because she had not grown up in it, so she was unlikely to trust or abide by its customs and mores. She would continue to flout the wealthy-folk rules of engagement with the legal system, and would never believe she or her daughter could get off scot-free.

"The policemen I've met," I said, "and I'm not pretending there have been a lot of them, all used to read Superman comics when they were little. They wanted to catch bad guys when they grew up. They feel compelled to make things safe for the good people."

"Some of them manage to get over that."

"I know, I know. Even so, I want to talk to Sally one more time. See if she'll listen to reason now that she knows we know the whole story."

"Do we?" he asked.

"Do we what?"

"Know the whole story."

"What else is there to know?"

"We know who was there when Victor died, and how he died," Thorne said. "I don't believe that's everything there is to know."

Of course he was right. Nobody ever knows everything about anything. What we think we know is filtered through our own expectations and bias.

It's like those subatomic particles whose location can never be fixed; the act of looking for them changes where they are. You can only guess at where they're likely to be. Looking at people and guessing what they're likely to do or be is nothing more than an exercise in creating our own reality for ourselves, based on our thin understanding of human nature in general and of any specific human in particular. And then folks fool you.

Thorne humored me. Instead of heading to the beach we drove to Presidio Terrace and stopped at the gate to the Avery mansion. He keyed in the code and nothing happened.

He looked at me. "She learns fast," he said.

He parked the car on the street and we walked to a six-foot stucco wall fronting the sidewalk on either side of a locked wrought-iron gate. Thorne put his hands on top of the wall and in a single motion hoisted himself up to sit on the wall, swung his legs over the top, and hopped down lightly to the lawn inside.

I had seen him use his hands and arms, but my impression was that he simply jumped. Jumped six feet in the air from a standing start. *Boing*, like he had springs in his shoes, and he was over. He pressed something on the inside of the pillar beside the gate and the gate clicked open.

"I take it your bullet wound is mending okay," I said.

"Actually, that hurt. I might have been showing off."

"For me?" I said, holding my hands together as if he had presented me with a bouquet of flowers. He tipped an imaginary hat.

At the front door he rang the bell. He gestured for me to stand behind him, out of sight. Lupita opened the door and said hello, and explained in Spanish *lo siento*, she was sorry, the senora had told her not to let him in.

He held his voice down and spoke in a kind of sing-song, the way you apologize to a child who isn't going to get ice cream after all, and I heard the words "*Natalia*" and "*policia*," and then Lupita asked him to *spere un momento* and closed the door.

We waited. I heard a lawnmower across the street and smelled new-mown grass. The mower stopped and its ugly drone was replaced by the flowing trill of a mockingbird, the grey bird singing its heart out, sitting on a power line next door.

Then the door opened and there was Sally. I stepped out alongside Thorne.

"*You!*" she raged. "When will you learn to mind your own goddamn business!" It wasn't a question.

"It's not something that can be dropped, Mrs. Avery. Natalie caused Victor's death."

"What do *you* care what happened? Why is this your problem?" she demanded. "Why can't you leave us alone?"

"Victor was my friend," Thorne said to her.

She shifted her attention to him, assessing him. He thought it was all he had to say to make his meaning clear, but to her he might as well have been speaking Martian.

"He was my husband. It's my business, not yours," she said, her cheeks red with anger.

"People can see us, Mrs. Avery," I said. "It would be better if we had this conversation indoors." I hoped my reminder of the pre-eminent WASP rule—never never *ever* under any circumstances make a scene—would cause her to invite us in.

"Fuck those people," she spat out. "*Fuck those people*," she yelled at the street. "There will be *no* conversation. There will be *no* police. Natalie was not here the night Victor was killed—the night he died." Her face fell at her blunder and she shook her head and put her hand up to her forehead.

"Ellis told us the whole story," I explained, resigned to standing on the front steps. "Including Natalie's theft of the ether from the plant, the fact that she had Victor's gun and took your car and the security video. The truth is going to come out, one way or another. That's what the truth always manages to do."

She lost her temper, and in her anger she forgot her unwillingness to talk. "Ellis blamed it on *Natalie*? Oh, he would, that snake. He raped me, you know. I was seventeen years old and he raped me. 'You know you want it,' he said. 'You knew what was going to happen when you came here to meet me. I'm not doing anything you don't want me to do.' It was horrible. So whatever he tells you, you keep in mind that he's a rapist and a blackmailer and a killer, and all he wants is to get back at Victor for things that happened when he was twelve years old or some crazy goddamn juvenile thing. Something normal people get over when they grow up and realize that everybody had a crappy childhood."

I wondered what must have gone through Sally's mind when Victor asked her to marry him. Perhaps Ellis wasn't the only one who had sought revenge; Sally's was just fatally misdirected.

"When I found out I was pregnant," Sally said, "I went looking for Ellis on campus. They treated me like I was scum. They said he'd gone home. One of his friends from that night in the restaurant came on to me and I pretended to go along with it so he'd tell me what happened. He said Ellis had been kicked out of school the day they came to the restaurant, and had flown home the next morning. He'd been kicked out for cheating. Big surprise. This asshole then proceeded to tell me he was more fun than Ellis, and could we go somewhere quiet. *Fun!*" She shook her head in amazement.

"Where did you find Natalie on the night Victor died?" I asked. "Where was she when you found her?"

I thought Ellis might not have given Sally a heads-up after we left him; he might be planning to clear out for Biloxi without any further contact. I didn't want Sally to realize we knew where Natalie was, in case I was going to have to call the police. If Ellis told Sally we were going to send the police to the Mark Hopkins, she'd move her daughter.

Still fuming, forgetting that she should not be talking to us, she said, "Natalie called me from Fort Mason. It was the middle of the night and the firemen and police had finally gone. She was driving my car and hers was at her friend's, and Thorne was somewhere with the Porsche, so I had to call a cab to take me to her."

She shook her head. "Natalie was scorched and bruised and crying. She told me Ellis was the one who brought the ether to the house and caused the explosion, and she said she took the car and ran because she was afraid he would come after her. It's not enough that he wrecked *my* life," she said. "He's doing his damnedest to wreck Natalie's too. I put her..." she caught herself in time.

"I put her someplace safe and arranged security for her," she said. "I got her a doctor and explained to the security people what they were there for, and I came home. I had just gotten home when you two walked in. Ellis called me yesterday and blamed Natalie, but she says he did it. Who am I supposed to believe?"

I said, "Natalie took canisters of ether from the plant before this, Mrs. Avery. She and Ellis have been plotting the company takeover for months, and you've been helping them. Nothing Natalie did was an accident. She is not just some troubled teen who needs to be grounded for a few days. She shot Thorne."

She stared dumbly at me, and then at Thorne. He lifted his shirt and showed her the bandage at his waist.

Slumping with exhaustion, or maybe it was resignation, she said, "I've got nothing more to say to either of you. Go away and don't come back," and she pushed the heavy front door shut in our faces.

≈21≈

I didn't know what to do next. I looked at Thorne, who shrugged. We walked out of the gate to the car and drove away from the lawn mowers and mockingbirds.

"Where to?" Thorne asked.

"For now, we head to Doctor P."

We drove to the dune-top parking lot at the end of Sloat Boulevard and sat looking out at the ocean. The sun was behind us, its light glancing across the endless water. Waves broke with a thump and hiss a quarter of a mile out.

We sat in amicable silence and watched the world. Standing at the tail bed of the pickup truck parked next to us, a surfer stripped off his wetsuit under a beach towel. To our left a dark-haired woman dried off a very wet, very happy black

Labrador retriever, the dog's tongue hanging out the side of his mouth, his thick tail wagging. He grabbed the towel in his teeth and started tugging. She growled at him and tugged back.

"What do you think?" I asked Thorne. "Natalie or Ellis?"

"Or both."

"Oh hell. Or both."

We looked out at the water and the waves. Seven miles up the beach, a massive container ship sailed out of the Golden Gate. From this distance it seemed barely to move, but within half an hour it would be beyond the horizon.

"I don't know what to do next, Thorne. I think people have done all the talking to me they're going to do."

"Someone will talk to you."

"Who?"

He pulled the detective's business card out of his shirt pocket and handed it to me.

"You want me to call the police? I thought that was against your principles."

"Victor was my friend."

I thought about Victor. Thorne was his steadfast ally, Chip Vronsich loved and admired him, Mater and her gal pals thought he was a good man. Sally had tricked him cruelly, Ellis resented him and was hell-bent on ruining him, and Natalie rebelled against him and may have killed him, if Ellis was telling the truth.

This was a crime, not an accident. I couldn't

remember when I had become a stickler about right and wrong, or even when it was that I decided I knew the difference between the two and was not a fan of situational ethics. But I did know the difference, and the difference mattered to me.

The image of the Fool Card came back to me; I saw the child reaching for the fruit, the young man heading for the cliff. What struck me was the apparent simplicity and goodness of their intention, the pure-heartedness with which they were initiating action. I thought that intention might be what dictates one's fate when embarking on some uncharted path.

"Natalie scared the bejesus out of me," I said. "More than Ellis. There was something truculent and unpredictable and toxic about her that was appalling. She may have had a right to be angry at her mother, but she was making choices that were all of them evil."

I thought some more. It was not enough for me to know what happened and just let events unfold as they would without my further involvement.

"All right," I said. "Let's find a pay phone."

At the zoo, which I considered a reasonably appropriate location from which to call the police and inform them about what I had learned about these people, I dialed the number on the business card.

Of course I reached voice mail. I left a detailed message without mentioning my name and I hung up. I used my scarf to wipe the handset and keypad off after I hung up, just in case.

Sitting in the car I told Thorne about leaving the message and said, "I need some time off, please. I need to sit and read and do nothing except sip tea."

"I have to take care of some things," he said. I didn't ask him what things. I thought it might involve doubloons.

"Do you need a car?"

"Helpful, but not essential," he said.

"How about if we drive to the first place you need to be, and I'll drive home from there, and you can find your own way after that? I'm a little fussy about lending the car."

"Deal."

We drove eastward on Sloat Boulevard. I wrestled with my personal history for a few minutes and then asked him, "Where will you go after this is over?"

"I don't know."

"You don't have another client?"

"No."

It was a struggle for me, both of us aware of what I was working my way up to. He let me struggle.

"Let's see what happens," I said, wimping out.

"Let's," he said, smiling his little smile.

I wished there were a Wounded Birds Anonymous and I could call my sponsor.

I let him out at Crocker's Lockers on Harrison Street and drove home. I sat on the carpet and petted all my pets and made tea and pulled *The City of Falling Angels* from the new-book shelf of the bookcase and tried to read about Venice. Instead my mind wandered over the experiences of the past few days.

How did I feel about what was happening? How tuned in to my own impulses and reactions and emotions was I? I have a long history of going numb when things become stressful. I believe I carry a dominant gene for stress-induced numbness.

I sat on my handsomely reupholstered couch and took stock. When the Fool Card shows up in a reading, it's a good idea to stop and assess what's happening from time to time, because things can careen out of control if you blink.

Life brings us unanticipated tests, and we do our best to cope. The Avery family's crisis had literally landed on my doorstep, and I had chosen to engage with it. Whether that was smart or stupid made no difference now. I felt like I had done everything I could or ought to do about the Avery family's dreadful situation, and I could release myself from any further sense of responsibility or guilt. I had been dragged into the mess and had willingly participated in the pursuit of truth, yes, but the final outcome would be out of my hands. So be it.

Also, I had met Thorne. Unlike the previous

times I had gone tearing around, inspired by yet another smart-but-hapless-guy rescue, I realized that with Thorne I did not feel ignored or undermined or at a loss.

No. I felt recognized and respected and happy. I wasn't besotted; I was at peace with myself. And I was confident things were different this time, since it had been two whole days and I hadn't yet given Thorne a house key.

Perhaps this relationship felt different because he appeared to have money of his own. My typical rescue cases are hilarious, intelligent, virile, charming, poetic, and penniless. In addition, they all have excellent hair, and I have no clue what that's supposed to mean.

Ask Sigmund. Or Euripides.

א א א

I wasn't sure what would happen next, and I didn't feel much satisfaction as a result of my phone call to the police. From nursery school on, we're told how unsavory it is to rat people out, and I admit I felt a tad unsavory, like I'd silently cut the cheese in a crowded elevator.

I put on a jacket, took my book with me, and sat in Sutro Park. I like the nasturtiums blooming along the pathways. How do they bloom in different colors—dark orange, bright yellow, red—all on the same plant? How do humans all learn the same values: do not kill, do not steal, do not lie, and then ignore those values with such avid brutality?

Sutro Park is a small quiet place, named for a Comstock Lode mining baron who later became mayor of San Francisco. The park is perched at the edge of the city, dark with the tall trees Sutro planted. It's usually foggy and generally empty.

I sat for a long time. Now and then I stood up and ambled around a little. As the afternoon stretched on, people came along walking their dogs. In the peculiar way of dog owner etiquette, I knew the dogs' names but not the owners'. Max and Sophie, Tyco and Sweetface and Snowy, Blue and Tupper and Kinky.

One owner, way too erudite or else trying to flash around his Mensa membership without mentioning it in so many words, has a pair of French bulldogs named Heidegger and Wittgenstein. I accept this philosophically and keep a trove of puppy biscuits in my jacket pocket. I call the bulldogs Martin and Ludwig because it makes the owner smile.

By four o'clock I was feeling a little better about things, and I was out of puppy biscuits and ready to go home. There, sitting on my front doorstep once again, was Thorne.

I let him in the house and in amicable silence we went about the business of making tea. He stood at the kitchen window opening a package of cookies and looking down at the street. I filled the kettle and plugged it in to boil. I heard a car coming fast up Anza Street toward the corner where my house sits.

"Turn off the kettle. Get the pets outside. Now!" he said, and before I could ask why he was out of the kitchen and down the stairs to the front door.

I looked out the window and there was a silver Jaguar in front of the house with the passenger door open. I grabbed the sleeping cats up out of their bed by their scruffs and called the dogs. They scrambled down the stairs with me and out into the side yard. I put the cats down and they clawed their way through the bark chips and crouched under the deck.

I heard Natalie Avery's voice raised in a rough shriek and Ellis yelling at her to get in the car.

I opened the side yard gate and stepped out into Sutro Park. Ahead of me at streetside the cement sidewalk cover to my house's gas line was tilted open and something that looked like an old-fashioned Thermos peeked up beyond the edge of the hole. I heard a rapid uneven snapping and saw bouncing around next to the silver canister the shredded red paper from an exploding double row of the little firecrackers you can buy in Chinatown.

Natalie was struggling to get loose from Thorne's grip on her and she was screaming for help. Ellis stayed in the car, shouting at her.

She was holding a pistol. I watched Thorne

put his massive hand around hers and lift the gun away from her as if giving it to him was precisely what she wanted to do.

Wisps of smoke were rising from the silver canister. Thorne let go of Natalie's arm and she ran to the car and climbed in. Before she even rounded the trunk of the car, Thorne used the toe of his shoe to flip the firecrackers away from the canister of ether.

As the firecrackers jumped around on the pavement, he bent and picked up the canister, and with a shout he threw it up and out over the park, away from my house, away from the Jaguar, away from everything but the sky and the trees and the fog that was flowing in from the Pacific on the four o'clock wind.

I lost sight of the canister against the gray sky and the fog; then there it was again, gleaming and spinning high in the air. It must have soared two hundred feet up before it arced and began to fall. From behind me I heard two pistol shots and I hunched down and crossed my arms over the top of my head.

There was a burst of orange and red and black and I shut my eyes and fell down onto the grass as a blast of sound and air pressure hit me. Hawk and Kinsey yelped and went down too, and then Hawk was looming over me, sniffing at me and licking my face.

I hadn't registered it while I was watching the canister fly higher than it seemed possible to throw it, but there had been a squeal of the Jaguar's tires. I glanced up.

Thorne, lowering the pistol he had used to explode the ether, turned and ran. "Ran" is an inadequate verb, actually. In three steps he was at full speed, flying up the hill after the Jaguar.

Hawk took off after him and, as rangy and fleet-footed as that big dog is, he was not gaining on Thorne, whose long legs were a blur.

By the time I was up on my feet Thorne was six houses away. I ran to the street, such running as I could manage by comparison, and he was three-quarters of the way down the block.

The light at Geary was red, and Thorne would have caught them had they stopped for it. I think if he had been chasing me, and I had the car doors locked and bulletproof windows rolled all the way up and an infallible cosmic death ray aimed at him, even then I'd have run the red light to get away from him.

So I wasn't surprised when Ellis did run the red light. He didn't knock off any pedestrians or cyclists. A white moving van, O'Malley's painted in green script on the side next to a shamrock, slammed into the Jaguar and the elegant silver car buckled inward on the passenger side and rolled up and over onto its ragtop roof.

The truck pushed the screeching upside-down Jag along for fifty feet before it could come to a halt, its front wheels resting on top of the car's undercarriage. After an awful couple of seconds, the truck rolled backward until all its wheels thumped down onto the pavement again.

The car's canvas roof and windshield had collapsed; the Jaguar's windowsills were flush with the pavement. The horn was blaring. The firecrackers next to my feet snapped and jumped on the sidewalk. Kinsey was barking beside me, and she kept barking. I could smell sulfur, and fog, and pine needles, and salt water, and an acrid whiff of ether. I held my breath.

Thorne stopped, turned, and into his arms he swept up Hawk, who weighs one hundred and twenty pounds. Hawk was barking, wriggling, anxious to be put down. Thorne bent his head and spoke quietly to the dog, and Hawk stopped squirming.

Putting Hawk down, Thorne held his collar and walked him along the sidewalk back to me. Hawk was capering, like a high-strung thoroughbred being led from his stall to the paddock before a race. Thorne had his hand held up to his side. There was blood showing on his shirt where the bullet wound had torn open. I let out my breath.

At the corner, two men climbed out of the moving van and edged up to the Jaguar. One man reached out and held on to the other man's shoulder, covering his mouth with his other hand. The two of them bent over to peer into the flattened car, but there was no way to see inside.

I took the pistol from Thorne, gripping it with

the bottom edge of my sweater, and carried it into my Japanese garden. I gouged a foot-long trough in the sand and dropped the pistol into it, smoothing the sand with my fingers and then raking it into grooves that matched the rest of the garden.

There were sirens in the distance. A flutter of ash settled around me; I could feel it brushing past my hair and face. I herded my dogs back into the house. The cats elected to bide their time under the deck. Hours would pass before they were good and ready to venture back inside. The fog swept in to scrub the smell and ashes away.

The big picture window facing the ocean was cracked but it hadn't shattered. Blood seeped through Thorne's shirt and his fingertips were torn where he had gripped the frozen canister, so I re-bandaged him and demanded that he lie down in the guest room, slathered with antibiotic goop and plastered with gauze and tape.

Sirens wailed on and off for hours. Police, ambulances, fire trucks, news vans, the coroner's wagon, tow trucks, all came and went during the evening and into the night. The dogs howled along with each new siren as it grew louder approaching the accident. I didn't tell them to shush. Once or twice I howled along with them.

Police officers knocked on everybody's door asking about the explosion, and I said it was shocking, and my window was broken and was going to cost a fortune to fix, and my pets were traumatized.

I had figured out that Detective Jackson must have called Ellis and/or Natalie. Thorne and I were the only ones who knew the whole story other than her mother, and Sally would never talk, so my guess was that Ellis and Natalie decided they could solve everything if they came after us and did to my house what they had done to Victor's library.

I was feeling a little resentful about it and I let my grumpiness surface in the way I spoke to the officer, pretending my rancor was the result of the broken window. I think he accepted that my tone was the result of the unanticipated insurance hassle rather than the attempt to blow my home up with me in it.

The officer told me a neighbor had mentioned seeing me with a tall man and a big dog, and I said I had been heading out to walk my dogs when the explosion caused one of my dogs to bolt.

I called Hawk, and when the dog came to the door the police officer held himself stiffly until I told Hawk to sit and Hawk actually sat. I told the officer the tall man had heard me calling the dog and caught him and brought him back to me. I said I didn't know the man's name; I had just thanked him and continued walking the dogs.

The policeman wrote down my name and number and went away. That was that.

≈22≈

The double funeral for Victor and Natalie Avery was three days later. The newspapers were still carrying front-page stories about the family, full of speculation about what really happened the night of the first explosion and the day of the second explosion and fatal car accident. Soon enough there were theories posted on the Internet that involved aliens.

My heart goes out to the men driving the moving van. There was a sidebar about them—about how the police had exonerated them from any blame for the deaths of Ellis and Natalie Avery, but they were still traumatized and would have to live with the terrible memory. One of them said he'd seen worse things during the Troubles, but nothing like so bad since he'd come to America.

I think about my father when I wonder how it affected Natalie to have the foundation of her beliefs about who her family was, who her father was, crumble around her.

I trusted my father completely when I was a child, but he abandoned me anyway. That he was an alcoholic, that his later behavior led me to bar him from my life, well, I'm not sure that, some decades and thousands of dollars in therapy later, I've come to terms with all of that—look at my wounded-bird history. But no matter how painful it is that my dad disappeared when he did, I can't imagine killing him for it. All Victor ever did was love and pamper Natalie, and he was as much in the dark about her parentage as she was.

There were articles in the business section about what might happen to Avery Chemical. An interim president was named and the press release assured the non-family shareholders that the company was doing well in spite of the tragedy.

There was a story about Ellis's family as well—about the share his widow now owned of the company and the change in her circumstances. It was quite a windfall. I imagine she feels something like I did after I got the legal settlement; everyone is congratulating her and she feels destroyed.

She has children, though. Maybe that will keep her steadier than I was able to be. She came to San Francisco to take Ellis's body back to Mississippi for burial. She refused to talk to reporters.

Whether or not the Averys would have accepted her, she knew enough about emulating old-money ways to shun publicity. Or maybe she was just a nice woman who preferred her privacy, and neither old nor new money had anything to do with her decision to thumb her nose at everyone and everything in San Francisco and take her husband home to the family that loved instead of hated him.

There were photographs of Victor's and Natalie's funeral in the paper, and there was television coverage that evening. The mass was celebrated at new St. Mary's, and my mother and her friends went. It was a day trip for Mater, so I didn't have to tell her the guest room was occupied.

Thorne went to the funeral. I hadn't known Victor, I could hardly claim to have known Natalie, and I was sure the last thing Sally wanted was to see me again, so I stayed home.

Thorne told me the mayor was there, and most of the Board of Supervisors, as well as all the big social wheels. They kept a tasteful and distinctly noticeable distance between themselves and the widow. No one patted her hand or whispered consolation to her as she sat with her parents in the front pew. No one walked her out with an arm around her shoulders supporting her in her grief, not even her father.

Victor's casket was blanketed with white tulips; Natalie's with baby pink roses.

I can't imagine what Sally was feeling. I suppose she felt terrible grief. But I can barely manage to notice what I'm feeling at any given time, much less what someone else is going through. And who knows what she was really thinking when she married Victor, or whether she thought Ellis would ever show up again.

Perhaps when she married Victor she thought it would all work out—that Victor would never learn who Natalie's father was, or if he did he might not care. Perhaps she thought it was only justice that one of the Averys should pay for what happened to her. But everybody wound up paying, including her, some of them paying the steepest possible price. Is the remaining money in Victor's estate enough to compensate Sally for the loss of her husband and daughter?

Maybe it is.

Since the funeral my mother tells me Sally has left town, sold the mansion, sold the other houses in Puerto Vallarta and Manhattan, sold her remaining shares of Avery Chemical to Bix Bonebreak, and disappeared. Nobody knows where she's gone. Nobody asks.

After a few days I pulled the pistol out of the garden and threw it into the Bay off Fort Point one evening. It flew high and far before splashing into the water under the Golden Gate Bridge.

Six weeks after the Avery deaths I saw Chip Vronsich's obituary. I went to his funeral with Thorne. It was at Glide Memorial, with the multiracial gospel choir singing "How I Got Over" and "All is Well with My Soul."

At Chip's request they took up a collection that would be split between AIDS research and feeding the many down-and-out folks who come to Glide every day for their only meal. Some days they run out of food before they run out of people. Many of the folks waiting in line to be fed are or have been addicts and are HIV positive. Many are just laid low by circumstances any of us could face.

Thorne and I don't talk a great deal, and about the Averys we talk not at all. Not that he ever talks much. We are content in our amicable silence, and we spent very little time working out whether he would stay in the guest room for the time being.

Here's how the negotiation went, in its entirety:

"Would you like to stay on downstairs?"

"Yes."

At his expense we rented a truck and bought cabinets and appliances and light fixtures and granite tile and plumbing supplies and wood flooring and lugged them back to my house.

I called in Marvin Schenk the handyman, and Phil Pan the plumber, and Sean Gilfoyle the carpenter-plasterer, and Remy Lopez the painter, and Bill Amhadan the Turkish electrician, and our little United Nations delegation installed an eat-in kitchen slash living room adjoining the bedroom.

There's no longer space to park a second, tandem car in the garage, but the Chrysler still fits, so okay.

I didn't get a permit from the city for the work, since it's a widely pursued municipal sport to build illegal in-law apartments on the ground floor of one's house.

Remodeling legally in San Francisco is like begging to be lashed to the mast and flogged, so the only people who do things legally are either related to the building inspectors, new in town, or afraid their neighbors will drop a dime on them. There is a reason for all the red tape; houses are built so closely together here that fire and earthquake codes need to be strict.

So we built the new room to code, but the city will still force me to tear it out if they discover it. I don't play the lottery; fixing up my house on the sly is a big enough gamble.

There's a new deadbolt on the door between the downstairs and the upstairs and I have the only key. Thorne being Thorne, he could undoubtedly lean on it with one pinky and it would crumble into splinters, but it's a door and represents a symbolic separation of powers. Of lives.

Thorne took it easy for a couple of weeks after the Avery death. The bullet wound mended steadily and he's now back to full Thorne-power.

He drove up in a dark grey BMW sedan a few days ago and parked it on the street, so I went to the Traffic Bureau to get a neighborhood parking decal for it. Otherwise the car would be plastered with tickets and at some point would get booted. He paid cash for the Beemer and it's registered in my name, in lieu of rent, Thorne says. Thus he remains an invisible man.

He's looking for a new client. He says he has heard that nobody holds it against him that his last client died. They all realize you can't protect someone from his immediate family if they live in the same house with him. Especially if the family consists of cheats, thieves, liars, blackmailers and addicts who tote around bombs in buckets.

Thorne and I don't visit back and forth too much, but we were drinking tea on the back deck yesterday, gazing at the Zen garden I had planted so tenderly, with its gray-green grasses and raked sand and round river rocks. Hawk and Kinsey were sleeping in the sun that shone down on all of us. Spring had finally arrived, and we could rely on experiencing some dawn-to-dusk sun for a few days here and there. Rain had stopped for the year but school was still in session, so the tourists had yet to arrive in huge volumes.

"How are you feeling?" he asked me.

"I'm taking it slowly."

I didn't pretend not to know what he was asking about.

"Factors?" he said.

"Do I want to live long-term with someone else in my house? That's the primary factor. If so, do I want it to be you? That's the secondary."

"The literal id in the basement."

"Just so. I seem to have consented to both, but I am still weighing the matter. And also I am weighing whether I want things to remain the way they are, if you get my drift."

"I do," he said.

We were amicably silent a little more.

"I like being the brawn to your brain," he said.

I smiled a little, hearing the Princeton graduate call me the brains. "I like it that you're open and straightforward. I like it that you're strong without being hard. You are the most feminine woman I've ever known, and it's got nothing to do with ruffles or pedicures."

I took in that he had spoken in multiple sentences. I held on and sipped some tea and did not cry.

When I could talk without my voice breaking I said, "I'm happy you don't require any repairs, literal or figurative, other than the occasional bullet wound. I like that you are utterly capable and self-sufficient and you are not intimidated by the fact that I am, too. I like working on things with you and feeling like we're one person with four arms. I feel safe around you, and it's got nothing to do with romance or dependency. Plus you have nice hair. Gigantic feet, but definitely good hair."

We sat in amicable silence some more.

"You know what it means when a man has big feet and big hands?" he asked.

I ignored him.

"Big shoes, big gloves," he said.

So he'll stay downstairs and we'll visit now and again. Our relationship remains uncategorizable, and I prefer it that way. I don't presume to speak for him.

I've informed the powers that be that I'm ready for what's next.

Because the readiness is all.

Bevan Atkinson, author of *The Tarot Mysteries* including *The Fool Card, The Magician Card, The High Priestess Card,* and *The Empress Card,* lives in the San Francisco Bay Area and is a long-time tarot card reader.

Bevan currently has no pets but will always miss Sweetface, the best, smartest, funniest dog who ever lived, although not everyone agrees with Bevan about that.

CPSIA information can be obtained
at www.ICGtesting.com
Printed in the USA
LVHW012346180822
726313LV00006B/96

9 780996 942508